"You belong to me, Elizabeth," Kelsey said fiercely.

She looked at his strong face through dazed eyes. "No," she whispered, distantly terrified of losing herself in the elusive complexity of this man. How could she belong to him when she didn't know who or what he was? How could she risk the most vulnerable part of herself by placing it in his keeping? No, she couldn't.

He held her eyes with his own, knowing he was walking a knife's edge, knowing he was moving too fast. But he had no choice. There was no time for the patience and rituals of courtship. "You know it's true, Elizabeth. Admit it."

She was confused, aching, frightened by the intensity of his demand and by her own instinctive urge to admit what he demanded. "No. I . . . I can't. I won't."

"You have to," he said. "Stop thinking and just feel. Your body knows you belong to me. Do you want me to prove it? If I carry you up those stairs, will you be able to say no?"

She closed her eyes, a ragged sigh escaping her lips. She knew the answer . . .

WHAT ARE *LOVESWEPT* ROMANCES?

They are stories of true romance and touching emotion. We believe those two very important ingredients are constants in our highly sensual and very believable stories in the *LOVESWEPT* line. Our goal is to give you, the reader, stories of consistently high quality that may sometimes make you laugh, sometimes make you cry, but are always fresh and creative and contain many delightful surprises within their pages.

Most romance fans read an enormous number of books. Those they truly love, they keep. Others may be traded with friends and soon forgotten. We hope that each *LOVESWEPT* romance will be a treasure—a "keeper." We will always try to publish

LOVE STORIES YOU'LL NEVER FORGET
BY AUTHORS YOU'LL ALWAYS REMEMBER

The Editors

LOVESWEPT® • 237

Kay Hooper
Unmasking Kelsey

BANTAM BOOKS
TORONTO • NEW YORK • LONDON • SYDNEY • AUCKLAND

UNMASKING KELSEY

A Bantam Book / February 1988

If you would be interested in receiving protective vinyl
covers for your Loveswept books, please write to this address
for information:

Loveswept
Bantam Books
P.O. Box 985
Hicksville, NY 11802

ISBN 0-553-21870-0

Published simultaneously in the United States and Canada

Bantam Books are published by Bantam Books, a division
of Bantam Doubleday Dell Publishing Group, Inc. Its trademark, consisting of the words "Bantam Books" and the
portrayal of a rooster, is Registered in U.S. Patent and
Trademark Office and in other countries. Marca Registrada.
Bantam Books, 666 Fifth Avenue, New York, New York 10103.

PRINTED IN THE UNITED STATES OF AMERICA

O   0 9 8 7 6 5 4 3 2 1

One

"Move it or lose it, buddy!"

If Kelsey had obeyed his common sense, he would have moved it. However, as the command woke him up quite abruptly from a sound, exhausted sleep, and as he was feeling a bit irascible because of it, he chose to force the issue. So, in his best Bogart imitation, he growled, "Scram!"

The wisdom of that response was instantly in doubt when he felt the cold hardness of a gun barrel against his neck.

In a matter-of-fact voice that was musical and yet held all the softness of an angry drill sergeant's, the woman said, "Any last words? A cigarette and a blindfold, maybe?"

Sitting very still, Kelsey chose to respond to the steely voice rather than the flippant words. "Uh—can we back up a little? I don't know who you are, but—"

"That makes us even, doesn't it? All I know is

that this piece of junk is parked on my land and you're in it. I get jumpy when strangers park on my land."

Kelsey wanted badly to turn his head and look at the woman, but didn't dare. "Look, I'm harmless," he insisted in his most bland and unthreatening voice. "I drove all night and I was tired, so I just pulled off the road to sleep. I didn't know this was private land."

"Now you do. Move it out."

"Did anybody ever tell you that you have a wonderfully light conversational touch?"

"I said beat it!"

She had her hand through the window in back, he realized, so, opening his door suddenly wouldn't throw off her balance. Then he caught a sudden glimpse of her hand in the rearview mirror, and he almost laughed. Instead, he reached over his shoulder abruptly and took her "gun" away from her. It was an empty soft drink bottle, and he stared at it in disgust.

Of all the childish tricks to be taken in by!

Muttering to himself, Kelsey tossed the bottle through the window, then opened his door and got out of the car. He fully intended to pour his wrath all over her, but when he turned and got his first look at his attacker, wrath was the last thing on his mind.

She stood confronting him, stiff and angry, magnificent green eyes blazing with temper. Her incredibly pale silver hair was piled atop her head in what he vaguely recognized as a chignon, with tendrils escaping to frame her face. And Kelsey had never seen such a stunningly beautiful woman in all his life.

No one—man or woman—would ever call her merely "pretty." She had the rarest kind of beauty, the beauty of bone structure and coloring that would remain with her all the days of her life. Her eyes were large and almond-shaped, fringed with long dark lashes, and their color was so vivid a green, they were almost iridescent. Her every feature was finely sculpted, and each blended so that her face was quite simply perfect.

"Close your mouth!" she snapped.

He did, then opened it again to laugh. "Damn, but you're lovely!" he said. And he was intrigued to note that not even a scowl could make her face less than beautiful.

She put her hands on her hips, continuing to glare. "Am I going to have to call the cops to get you off my land?" she demanded.

Kelsey was trying to ignore the effect she was having on his senses, which was rather like trying to ignore a tornado while standing just under the funnel. "Um, you just might," he confessed, feeling somewhat dazed. And in the back of his mind, behind all the rational, logical reasons why he just couldn't, not now, a little voice was groaning, *Oh, hell, what lousy timing!*

She blinked, and humor shone briefly in her eyes before temper rose up again. She turned her head and whistled sharply between her teeth.

Her teeth were lovely, too, he noticed. And the jeans and T-shirt she wore did absolutely nothing to hide the fact that nature had been as wonderfully generous below her neck as above. Kelsey decided he was dreaming. He decided he didn't want to wake up. Then he became aware that something was growling near his left hip, and he tore his gaze from her to look down.

He woke up. In a hurry.

It was disguised as a dog, but from the sound it was making, Kelsey deduced that it was either a grizzly bear or a Tasmanian devil. Its fangs looked perfectly capable of devouring a whole steer, a redwood tree trunk, or Kelsey's leg—which was what was closest at the moment.

Careful to keep his voice mild, Kelsey asked, "What the hell is that?"

"My dog. His name is Lobo. That means wolf. Lobo doesn't like strangers, either. Now, unless you can show me a badge—state or federal—and a warrant, along with a gun big enough to frighten Lobo, you'd better clear out."

"Right." He edged carefully back into his car and shut the door with absolute quiet, but then hesitated. Looking at the face he knew he'd never forget if he lived to be a hundred, he said quietly, "At least tell me your name."

She stood with one hand on the bristling ruff of her dog and stared at him for a long moment. "Elizabeth Conner," she said, and seemed surprised that she'd said it.

"Thank you. My name's Kelsey," he told her, and then started his car and drove away.

The town was named Pinnacle, and it had never lived up to its christening. A sleepy little village with a city limit that was about a mile long and half as wide, it was tucked away in the countryside like a trail forgotten by time. The nearest interstate highway was ten miles away, the nearest city of any size a hundred, and if it was on any state map, it boasted only a pinprick with which to mark its location.

But as Kelsey drove his battered Ford slowly through two caution lights on Main Street, he decided that Pinnacle had, somewhere, an ace up its sleeve. He had spent nearly two hours driving all around Pinnacle before venturing in, and from that had concluded that the town would be a stagnating, dying one.

There appeared to be few income-producing resources in the rural county. Scant acres of usable, productive farmland, no river or stream of any size, nothing to attract tourists, one lone industrial plant called Meditron operating about five miles from town, and if a company or private individual was cutting timber, it was well-hidden.

So Kelsey had expected a dying town, one being slowly choked to death by its own limitations. He expected to see few young people, no new businesses or construction, and signs of decay everywhere.

He was wrong on all counts.

The downtown area boasted several establishments of considerable size, all in excellent repair and, judging by traffic along the busy sidewalks on a weekday, flourishing nicely. At a rough estimate the population on the streets today had a median age of thirty and an income way above average, leaving folks with a lot of money to spend on themselves. Most of the cars on the picturesque street were late models, and there wasn't a weed, a broken-down building, or crooked street sign anywhere to be seen.

"Damn," Kelsey murmured. He continued down the main street and out of the downtown area, looking left and right to study some fine old homes and tasteful new ones, a compact little shopping center doing brisk business, an obviously new high school, and other signs of a healthy economy.

A county sheriff's patrol car cruised past in the other lane, and Kelsey looked in the rearview mirror and watched as it pulled into a parking lot, backed out again, and fell in behind his own car.

"Double damn," he muttered. It could have been coincidental, of course, but he doubted it. Kelsey didn't have a great deal of faith in coincidence. And he remembered, then, that Elizabeth Conner had ordered him off her land unless he could produce a badge—"state or federal." So, didn't the beautiful, bristly lady trust the local police? Now, that was interesting.

That was interesting as hell.

Kelsey found a small, neat motel about two miles from the city limits and pulled in there, nearly rammed head-on by a flashy sports car that was exiting at the same moment. Hanging his head out the window, he roared a few choice expletives, saw a faintly apologetic salute from the other driver, and parked his car with half his attention on that task and half on the patrol car that had departed, siren wailing, after the sports car.

He grinned a little, then got out of his car and went to acquire a room for himself. The result was a room, no more and no less; it was neat and clean and impersonal, and he barely glanced at the bland colors and sturdy furniture before dumping his bag and busying himself in showering and shaving.

He hardly looked at the face in the steamed mirror while he shaved automatically, but thought instead about everything he had seen and the conclusions he had reached. And he told himself that Elizabeth Conner figured prominently in those thoughts only because she looked like a good place to start. That was all, of course.

Sure it was.

Kelsey changed into clean clothes, faintly amused at himself for even thinking to check the shine of his shoes before leaving his room. He returned to his car, chose a less public road to leave the small town, and made only one stop before finding his way back to the place he had parked for sleep that morning. He took the precaution of parking his car out of sight behind a thicket of brambles, then moved cautiously up the dirt road, which led to a sprawling farmhouse in the distance.

He was automatically taking stock as he went, noting that all the acreage on one side of the dirt drive was given over to a flourishing orchard; peaches, he guessed uncertainly, since he wasn't familiar with the spring blossoms covering the short, gnarled trees planted in neat rows. On the other side of the drive was pastureland surrounded by a barbed wire fence; there was an elusively bare look to that land, as if little time or money had been spent in cultivating the thick stand of grass there. From that evidence, he concluded the pasture was not a money-making proposition, but merely used for the three or four horses he could see in the distance near a tumbledown barn.

Kelsey was still a good hundred yards away from the sprawling white house when he was confronted by the growling, clearly hostile Tasmanian devil disguised as a dog. Promptly, he sat down in the middle of the dusty drive, reached into the paper bag he carried, produced a large soup bone, and began talking to Lobo.

"Yes, but who *was* he?"

Elizabeth brushed a strand of silvery hair from her hot brow and frowned at her younger sister. "I didn't ask, Ami. Just some man who pulled off the road to sleep. Now, would you please stop waving that knife around and use it on the potatoes?"

Ami, who at fourteen was coping with the physical uproar of adolescent hormones and who was glumly convinced she was the ugliest creature since the proverbial duckling, looked at the older sister who had virtually raised her and felt depressed. Not that *any* woman, she thought vaguely, wouldn't be depressed when she looked at Beth.

Wielding her knife efficiently, Ami sent sidelong glances at her beautiful sister and thought disjointedly that Beth shouldn't be stuck way out here in the middle of nowhere. She should be a model, or actress . . . or . . . or a *queen*. There should be a gallant prince for her, one who wouldn't mind baby sisters with a lot of growing left to do before they could leave the nest. A prince with broad shoulders and a laugh in his eyes, one who could carry Beth's burdens and take away that awful strained look in her eyes.

A prince who would punch Blaine Mallory in the nose.

"Ami."

"Hmmm?" Dwelling on the lovely vision, Ami blinked and saw her sister holding up a potato denuded of much more than its skin. "Oh, I'm sorry, Beth, I just—"

"I know." Elizabeth smoothed her sister's long pale hair and smiled a little. "Daydreaming. But could you keep your mind on this until we get supper finished, sweetie?"

"Okay." Ami was intensely grateful that Beth never made fun of her daydreaming, or her constant bouts with awkwardness as she tried to adjust to the added inches that had come upon her with startling suddenness. And Beth never got mad at her for blurting out whatever popped into her head, like when she had asked Blaine Mallory why he smiled with his teeth but never his eyes.

If she *had* to have a gorgeous sister, at least she was glad it was Beth. Now, Meg, on the other hand—

"I see the chickens are going to get a lot more potato than skin again, half-pint. Where does your mind go?"

Ami bristled instantly. "It was *your* turn to do this, Meg, but you had to parade those shorts of yours in town hoping Jeff Mallory would see!"

"That's enough," Elizabeth said mildly before Meg could voice the retort hovering hotly on her lips. "Here, Meg, take this and set the table, please." She handed her younger sister a handful of silverware, meeting the mutinous blue-green eyes steadily until Meg turned away with a flounce.

Under her breath, Ami muttered, "The whole town's talking about her, Beth."

Elizabeth sent her a small smile, but said nothing. Still, Ami could see the increased worry in her sister's eyes when they rested on Meg, and it infuriated her. What was *wrong* with Meg, adding to Beth's troubles like she did? She seemed hellbent to prove she was as beautiful as her sister, and it just wouldn't happen. Not that Meg wasn't pretty, Ami decided with reluctant fairness. She was. She had the pale hair of all the sisters, and her blue-green eyes would be lovely if only they weren't so sulky, and her face was delicate. Her figure was good, too, except that she insisted on dressing it scantily in shorts, tops, and jeans that were indecently tight.

She was sixteen, and certainly old enough to know how dangerous her games were. She flitted from one boy to another, reckless, dissatisfied with them after a short while. She wore too much makeup and swore too much, and she both drank and smoked when she was out of Beth's sight. She thought Beth didn't know. Idiot, Ami decided irritably. Of course Beth knew.

"Are the potatoes ready, sweetie?"

Ami handed over the peeled and sliced vegetables, and she felt absolutely wild for a moment. They were increasingly common, these violent emotions; she often burst into tears when something upset her, astonished by her own lack of control. It would get better in time, Beth had told her gently. When her mind and emotions caught up with her maturing body, it would get better.

But for now, she made an incoherent sound

and then said intensely, "I have to go outside,
Beth! I can't *stand* it when Meg acts like this! I
just can't!"

"All right, honey." Beth smiled at her, understanding. "But don't go far. Supper in half an
hour."

Ami nodded, rushing out the back door as if
some demon pursued her, and managing to make
it around the corner of the house before she burst
into tears. She swiped at the wetness angrily as
she stalked toward the driveway, feeling so frustrated and worried that she didn't know where to
turn. She couldn't tell Beth about part of it, because her sister would only worry more if she
knew that Ami had overheard a few conversations
she shouldn't have and had guessed what was
going on; Beth, as always, was trying to shield
her younger sisters, and had accepted the burden
onto her own shoulders.

And it just wasn't *right*, dammit!

"Hello."

Ami nearly jumped out of her skin. She looked
up—a long way up—and felt her breath catch on a
last sob. Heavens, but the man was big! He reminded her of a soldier she had seen once, large
and powerful but with a way of moving and even a
way of standing that made you forget he was huge.
And he had a lean face that was smiling, a not
really handsome face but oddly pleasant. His hair
was a rusty shade of brown and his friendly eyes
were a color somewhere between blue and gray.
And even though Ami felt—*knew*—instantly that
here was the prince she had hoped for, a shrewd
part of her mind was wary.

Kelsey had seen the girl bolt around the corner of the house as if she were running from something, and he had had a few moments to take stock as she approached him. Definitely a sister, he had decided; she was too old to be a daughter—fourteen or fifteen, he guessed. Her slender body showed hints of womanhood but was still ungainly in the transition of adolescence. Her long hair was pale and baby-fine, her thin little face filled with the sharp angles that promised later beauty in bone structure but presently made her features ill-matched; she would be as lovely as her sister, he knew, within a few years.

"Hello," he offered, intentionally low-key and friendly. And he studied her as she stood staring at him. Haunting eyes, he thought, more blue than green and presently anxious beneath the surprise. She stood poised like a startled fawn, and he felt a curious and unaccustomed gentleness soften something deep inside him.

She was just a baby, a worried and anxious baby troubled by more than the chaos of her maturing self.

"I was here this morning," he went on in the same low, pleasant tone, seeking to ease her wariness. "Your sister—must be your sister—ran me off. Elizabeth?"

"Yes." Her voice was soft, curiously wondering. "Beth. I'm—I'm Ami."

The instant he heard her voice, his eyes narrowed briefly, but his own voice remained friendly. "Hello, Ami."

"Why did you come back?" she asked, not as if she didn't know the reason, but as if she wanted confirmation of some private deduction.

Kelsey debated briefly, but found that no inner decision was necessary. Honestly, he said, "I wanted to see Elizabeth again. I think she's worried about something, and I want to help her."

Ami's wide gaze dropped to bemusedly watch his fingers moving in the ruff of the big dog beside him. "You made friends with Lobo? He's always hated men. He bit Blaine once," she confided with an air that was half pleasure and half guilt.

"Blaine?" His interest quickened; it looked as though his Irish luck had come through yet again.

Ami chewed her lower lip, her gaze returning to his face. Instead of responding to his question, she asked one of her own. "Who are you?"

"My name's Kelsey, Ami."

She didn't appear to find the answer lacking. "Kelsey. I like that. Would you stay for supper, Kelsey?"

Laughter leapt to his eyes. "I'd love to. But don't you think we should ask Elizabeth about that?"

There was a stirring gleam of amusement in her own eyes, as if she were hugely enjoying herself. "It's my house too. You'll be my guest, okay?"

"Okay." He accepted the slender little hand that reached trustfully for his own, vaguely conscious that this was hardly something he had bargained for. This little fawn had seemingly adopted him with startling swiftness, and he couldn't help but believe that her older sister was not going to like it. Still, it was incredibly lucky that he had stumbled into just the place he needed to be.

"Why were you crying, Ami?" he asked as they walked toward the house with Lobo pacing silently beside them.

"Because I'm a teenager," she said baldly with a rueful shake of her head. "I cry over *everything*. But Beth says I'll grow out of it. I just hope it's soon."

Both amused and sympathetic, he said, "It's rough, isn't it? You feel like yelling or crying, and your body doesn't want to work right and nothing fits anymore."

She looked up at him, grateful. "Yes! Just like that. And I suppose one *has* to go through it, but it's terrible."

He smiled down at her. "You live here with your parents?"

Ami shook her head. "Our parents were killed in a car crash ten years ago. I was just four, so I hardly remember them. Beth raised me—and Meg, who's sixteen. I guess she raised Jo too; Jo's twenty-three now and doesn't live at home much anymore." She frowned broodingly, her anxiety increasing. Then she shook off whatever disturbed her. "I'm glad Beth was old enough then to convince the judge we didn't need anyone else, but she was only sixteen. It hasn't been easy for her." Ami looked up at him with faint entreaty. "So if she snaps at you—or acts all prickly like brambles— you'll remember that, won't you? That it hasn't been easy for her?"

"I'll remember, Ami," he told her gently, and thought to himself that "Beth" had done a good job in raising this one. "So there are four of you?"

"Uh-huh."

Something tugged at him. "Your names . . . there's something familiar about them."

"*Little Women.*" Ami grinned. "I doubt you read

the book; most men won't admit to it even if they did. But you probably saw one of the movies. We weren't named in order, since Beth is older than Jo, but Mama loved that book. I think she changed the order because she was superstitious; Beth died in the story, you know."

He remembered then. "Of course. I did see a movie."

"We get teased sometimes," Ami confided. She led him up onto a wide front porch and through the door into the house, allowing the dog to come in with them.

It was a comfortable house. Old enough to possess the rabbit warren of small rooms that had been common when it was built, it had clearly been remodeled within the past few years. The rooms were large and airy, with pale walls and shining wood floors dotted here and there with thick rugs. The color scheme was mostly pastels, cool blues, and greens with occasional splashes of brighter colors. There was a great deal of quiet taste in the decorating, and Kelsey's shrewd eyes saw also that whoever had done the house had been working with a limited budget and had done wonders with the place.

Then he was being led into a bright kitchen, and Kelsey found himself confronting the beautiful Elizabeth. She turned from a stove from which appetizing scents wafted, and froze the moment she saw him.

And Kelsey had a conflicting set of impressions and feelings. She was, he saw, even more beautiful than he remembered. Even obviously hot and a little tired, she was lovely. Strands of silver hair

clung to her damp brow and throat, her irridescent green eyes were wide and angry, her magnificent body stiff. She didn't want him here, didn't
want him here at all, he realized, and this was
where he had to be. Where he suddenly wanted to
be—and not for professional reasons.

As with Ami, he could see an underlying anxiety in her eyes, and there were hints of strain he
hadn't noticed before; at that first meeting, he'd
been too overwhelmed by her to see much more
than surface beauty. But now he saw. He saw the
evidence of stress on her face, the faint shadows
beneath her eyes and the look of utter control
holding her features. He saw a mouth innately
curved with humor but held in a tight line, saw
from the fit of her jeans that she had lost weight
recently.

He wanted to help her. Suddenly, more than he
had ever wanted anything in his life, he wanted to
help her.

"Hi," he said lightly.

Before Elizabeth could utter a word, Ami said
firmly, "This is Kelsey, Beth. You remember him
from this morning. I've invited him to supper."

After a moment, Elizabeth said, "Ami, Meg went
up to her room. Could you go and tell her supper's ready, please?"

Her younger sister hesitated, then nodded. And
the glance she left Kelsey with was full of entreaty.
Unconsciously, he braced himself and returned
his gaze to Elizabeth.

"What do you want?" she asked tautly the moment Ami vanished.

All Kelsey's instincts told him that this woman

would not be put off with vague reasons. So he folded his arms across his chest, leaned back against the doorjam, and met her eyes squarely. "I want to know," he said quietly, "why you distrust the local police. I want to know what it is you're worried stiff about." He reflected for a moment, seeing her tension increase. "I want to know who Blaine is, and why Ami was happy that Lobo bit him."

"Get out of here."

As if he hadn't heard, Kelsey went on. "I've come to a few conclusions on my own. I drove through Pinnacle today. I have a room there, by the way. And I was absolutely fascinated to see what should be a dying town flourishing. Obviously, it's a company town, and obviously the company pays well. But it's odd, Elizabeth Conner, because that company isn't very well known."

"I said—"

"Doesn't look all that big, either." Seeming to ignore her interruption, he was watching her intently. "Meditron, a company listed as manufacturing medical equipment. Their books show a modest profit, nothing spectacular. I drove by there today. They have a surprising amount of security; it isn't exactly usual for armed guards to man an entrance gate for such a small company—unless they're doing something inside that they don't want people to know about."

"That has nothing to do with me," she said tightly. "I don't work at Meditron."

"I know." He ventured a small smile. "You raise peaches and sisters. I haven't met the other two, but it's obvious Ami is worried to death because *you* are worried. Now, since this is a tight-knit company town with the local law enforcement quite probably company-owned, I have to wonder."

"Who are you?" she whispered.

After a moment, he shrugged. "If I told you who I worked for, it wouldn't mean anything to you. We aren't listed in the phone book and don't offer guided tours of the home office. We're—uh, troubleshooters, for want of a better word. We got a tip that something was rotten in Pinnacle. A call from a distraught young lady was recorded by the FBI—the Washington office, by the way. It seems she wasn't even sure of the state boys, so she called the national office. She was too frightened to leave her name, and she was virtually incoherent. But it was clear she was worried about something going on at Meditron. They were doing bad things out there, she said. And she said other things. That they were hurting people. Particular people."

Elizabeth was frowning a little, wariness in her eyes.

"The matter was passed on to us," Kelsey went on. "I got the job. Turning up on your doorstep was a piece of luck I hadn't counted on."

Her frown deepened. "I told you, I don't—"

"Ami made the call, Elizabeth."

She went white. "That's crazy! Ami is fourteen, and she never goes around Meditron. She wouldn't know—"

"No," Kelsey agreed softly. "She wouldn't know, would she? Unless she had . . . overheard something? Unless she was convinced that your anxiety was tied up with Meditron. Unless she had realized what had happened to worry you so. Where's your other sister, Elizabeth? Where's Jo?"

She was utterly still, dead white, and there was anguish in her eyes. Then it was gone, and she was in control again. "Get out of my house," she said flatly.

"Let me help you."

"Get out."

Kelsey drew a deep breath and released it slowly. "And if I did leave? I'm still on this job, Elizabeth, I still have to find out what's going on, whether you help me or not. It's what I *do*. I stick my nose into things and I turn over rocks to see what crawls out from under them. I shake the cage until something rattles loose. And if your sister's in that cage, she could get hurt." He paused. "Of course, you could stop me. You could call Meditron—or Blaine Mallory; he runs the place, doesn't he? You could call him and warn him about me."

"Stop it," she whispered.

He could see she was trembling suddenly, and it hurt him. Unconsciously, his voice deepened and gentled. "Don't you see that I have to know how your sister is involved in this? I have to know, Elizabeth, so I can help her too. If you don't tell me, I'll have to find out for myself—and she could get hurt. I don't want that."

"I can't tell you anything," she said from between stiff lips. "Anything at all."

"You're too damned independent for your own good," he said softly. "Too proud to ask for help. Or is it something else? Are they holding Jo somewhere as a hostage, Elizabeth? Is that it? Have they threatened her if you don't keep quiet?"

"Please leave."

"You can't go it alone, don't you see? It's obviously tearing you apart. And there's Ami. She's worried too. And maybe your other sister knows more than you think. If it's blackmail, I can help; if they're holding Jo, I can help."

"You're a stranger." She spoke in the same soft, stiff voice.

"Yes. So you'll have to decide to trust me, won't you? Trust me, and let me help you."

A door banged sharply at the front of the house.

"Beth?" a deep masculine voice called briskly.

Kelsey glanced over his shoulder, then quickly at Elizabeth.

"It's Blaine," she murmured, a riot of emotions in her eyes.

Taking two quick steps to stand before her, Kelsey reached to grasp her shoulders and draw her stiff body into his arms. "Trust me," he whispered, and covered her startled lips with his own.

He could feel her resistance at first in the tautness of her muscles, feel her hands come up to his chest as if she would have pushed him away. Her eyes were wide at first, panicked. But then he felt a shudder pass through her. Her dark lashes slowly veiled the irridescent green eyes, and the tension drained from her body.

And in the space of a heartbeat, Kelsey's half-formed plan became less professional and much more personal. He stopped thinking about knocking Blaine Mallory off balance and flaunting his own presence innocently as a man interested in Elizabeth Conner. He stopped thinking about all the possibilities in this situation, the overtones and undercurrents of danger. He stopped thinking of why he was here. He stopped thinking.

Some distant part of him admitted silently that he had wanted to kiss her, and never mind professional needs.

She was warm and soft in his arms, her body melding bonelessly against his with no more than a slight pressure from his hand at the small of her back. Her mouth came alive in an instant, opening to him, her arms sliding slowly upward until her fingers lost themselves in his hair. And he pulled her suddenly even tighter against him, everything forgotten but the need to feel her body close to his.

Two

"Dammit, Beth, will you call off this brute of yours—" The man's voice broke off abruptly.

Kelsey, drowning in sensation, didn't want to hold his head above the water. And the woman in his arms seemed utterly unconcerned about having an audience. He heard the sound of footsteps, a jerky feminine exclamation, and a startled giggle from Ami. He also heard a vicious, suppressed sound from a man.

Slowly, he lifted his head, staring down into Beth's vivid eyes and wondering distantly if he looked as dazed as she did. Probably. He didn't give a damn about it, though. And then he heard Ami's innocent voice.

"That's Kelsey, Blaine. He came to see Beth."

And Kelsey heard a deep growling sound, along with the visitor's voice, distracted but still vicious.

"Somebody call off this damned—"

"Lobo," Kelsey murmured, allowing one hand to

leave Elizabeth and fall to his side. Almost immediately, he felt the thick ruff of the dog beneath his hand. And he didn't know if it was sheer, primitive male instinct that had made him show his mastery over the dog to the other man. Probably.

Elizabeth was drawing slowly away from him, a wave of faint color sweeping up her throat. She looked shocked, confused, and he touched her cheek with gentle fingers before he allowed her to leave his arms. It was up to her now.

In a soft voice she said, "I didn't expect you, Blaine." She was still gazing at Kelsey.

"Obviously!" Blaine snapped.

She blinked, but seemed unconcerned by his anger. "Blaine, this is—Kelsey. Kelsey, Blaine Mallory."

Kelsey turned slowly to face the other man. He saw a man about his own height but a good twenty pounds lighter. A strikingly handsome man somewhere in his thirties with jet black hair, a lean face, and an obvious habit of dressing well. A man with chilly blue eyes and a face whose muscles were tightly held in anger. Still absently petting Lobo, Kelsey said casually, "Hello. A friend of the family?"

Blaine's nostrils flared slightly, then he seemed to dismiss Kelsey as if he were less than human. "Beth, I want to talk to you," he said sharply.

In a polite tone, Kelsey said, "We're about to sit down to supper, you know. Much better if you come back later. And call first next time, will you?"

"I'll show you out, Blaine," Ami said brightly, sending Kelsey a quick look brimming with satisfaction.

Blaine opened his mouth to speak, but when Kelsey put an arm around Elizabeth and she came to him as if she belonged at his side, his mouth closed with a snap and he turned on his heel to stalk back through the house with Ami helpfully following.

Kelsey looked at the other sister, who was staring at him with her mouth open. She was a typical teenager, her clothes too tight and her makeup lavishly applied with a less than expert hand. She was also a pretty girl with a discontented expression and sulky blue-green eyes, and Kelsey guessed shrewdly that she was less surprised at his presence than displeased to find her sister in the arms of *any* man.

"Hello. You must be Meg," he said casually. "Why don't you and Ami wait for us in the dining room, okay?"

"I—" Meg turned abruptly and left the room.

Elizabeth pulled away from him again. "I—I don't understand." Her voice was shaking.

Kelsey knew only too well that she was fighting to resurrect her barriers, shocked by him and by herself, quite literally knocked out of kilter by what had happened. And no wonder, considering all she must have been through before today. He took her hand gently, pulling her around to face him again, and his free hand lifted to touch her hot cheek.

"I know. I also know," he added with intentional dryness, "that you probably would have slapped my face under ordinary circumstances. But the circumstances aren't normal for you, are they? You're tired and tense, and undoubtedly scared—and I took advantage of that. I'm sorry,

Elizabeth. Not for kissing you. I could never be sorry about that. Just for the timing, that's all."

She was looking up at him, baffled and uncertain. Not yet balanced enough to be embarrassed. "You . . . you acted like you wanted Blaine to think—"

"Yes, I did. I wanted him to think I was interested in you. Maybe even that I had a prior claim. That is what he has in mind, isn't it?"

In a low voice, she said, "He wants me to marry him. His persistence is like water dropping on a stone."

"Is he threatening Jo to blackmail you?" Kelsey asked bluntly.

She winced, but shook her head. "No. He doesn't think he has to be underhanded or ruthless about it. He thinks he can—can have me any time he really tries."

Kelsey was a fairly even-tempered man, not given to emotional outbursts and certainly trained and experienced enough to control what he did feel. He was a little surprised at himself that he should feel a definitely savage urge to go after Blaine Mallory and beat the hell out of him. But he leashed those emotions, aware that Elizabeth couldn't take much more, at least not today. Cheerfully, he said, "Well, then, I'll just be your buffer."

She had regained some of her control, and looked at him with misgivings. "And what will I be?" she asked warily, drawing her hand from his as if she had just noticed.

Honestly, he said, "You'll be a buffer for me. A reason for me to be here, unconnected with Meditron." And so much more, so much that he hadn't planned on.

Elizabeth turned away and began automatically to transfer the food from cooking pots to serving dishes. "I don't know what to believe," she murmured. "I can't trust you. I just can't!"

"Yes, you can," he insisted quietly, beginning to help her. "You have to, Elizabeth. If you don't want to tell me about your sister yet, then we'll wait on that; we have a little time, I think. Mallory isn't suspicious of me, and won't be if we get our story straight—"

"What story?"

He saw her hands shaking, and gently took a serving dish from her. Forcing his voice to remain casual and cheerful, he said, "The story of how we met, of course. Mallory has to believe I came out here to court you, and he's bound to ask you questions. So we'll come up with something to satisfy his curiosity—and Meg's, since I could see she didn't think much of me. Ami will be easy, I believe."

Elizabeth almost smiled. "She likes you. Meg . . . Meg is going through a rough period right now. She's rebelling. Both of them missed having a father . . ." Her voice trailed into silence.

"Well, maybe they can use a big brother," he observed in the same light tone. "I'll see what I can do."

Her face closed down suddenly. "No," she said evenly, "don't do that. It'll be worse for them when you're gone."

Kelsey watched her for a moment as she piled warm rolls into a linen-lined wicker basket. "Where could we have met?" he asked, thinking it wiser to change the subject. And he almost held his breath, hoping either that Mallory had become too insistent for her to feel confident about fighting him, or else that she realized she really needed his help in this situation. Whatever. As long as she accepted him.

She was silent for a moment, then shrugged jerkily. "Charleston, I suppose. I go there sometimes. Shopping and just to get away."

"Charleston it is, then. I'll take those." He took two of the dishes from her, then followed as she led the way to the dining room, more relieved by her response than he had expected. *Damn* Hagen, he thought distractedly. Intentionally or not, it looked as if his boss had borrowed Cupid's bow again. The man really ought to abandon his federal machinations and open up a dating service.

"Just who the hell are you?" Meg demanded angrily the moment he came into the small dining room.

Kelsey ignored the faint sound of protest from Elizabeth. He pulled her chair out for her, then took one for himself and smiled easily across the table at the angry girl. "I'm Kelsey, and I came to Pinnacle to visit your sister," he told her calmly.

"It's funny we never heard of you before," Meg said suspiciously, her sulky eyes narrowed.

Ami opened her mouth, then intercepted a look from Kelsey and shut it, addressing herself to the meal.

Cheerful, Kelsey said, "Maybe she didn't think I was worth mentioning. I came out here to prove her wrong, though."

"Meg, please," Elizabeth said in a low voice.

Kelsey could hear the strain, and the smile he sent Meg then was underlaid with steel. "We won't talk about it right now," he said gently.

Meg glared at him, but nonetheless began eating without further comment. And after a gleeful look at Kelsey, Ami began talking casually about the events of the previous school week. She fetched more ice tea from the kitchen when it was needed, even pouring some for Meg with the long-suffering look that only a fourteen-year-old could perfect. And Ami kept talking lightly, seeming not to notice Elizabeth's silence or the frequent glances Kelsey directed to her bent head.

When Kelsey realized that Elizabeth was just going to keep shoving the food around on her plate without eating much of it, he pushed back his chair and went around to hers. "Come on," he said softly. "We'll go sit on the porch swing for a while. The girls can clean up."

"I have a call—" Meg began to wail, but Ami's sharp kick under the table silenced her.

"Of course we will. You go on, Beth." Ami smiled sunnily.

Silently, Elizabeth allowed Kelsey to pull out her chair, and she led the way from the house and onto the front porch. She sat down in the swing, stiffening slightly when Kelsey joined her, but not looking at him.

After a moment, Kelsey said, "The FBI got that call over a week ago. How long has it been, Elizabeth? How long have you been under this kind of pressure?" And, when she didn't respond, he sighed. "Long enough. You haven't had a decent night's sleep or a good meal in too long."

Elizabeth stiffened even more when he put an arm around her and drew her head to rest on his shoulder. But his voice was inexpressibly soothing when he murmured, "Sleep, Elizabeth. You're not alone now. I'll keep the villains at bay with my trusty sword, I promise."

She almost smiled. He was moving the swing gently, creating a soft breeze and a soothing motion, and his hard body was a curiously comfortable resting place. Too tired to think anymore, she gradually relaxed, and soon her eyelids became too heavy to hold open. Finally, she slept.

Kelsey held her gently, moving the swing automatically and gazing off into the deepening twilight. It had all just caught up with her today, he realized. He had seen too much strength in the angry woman of this morning to believe that she was knocked off balance very often, or for very long. He doubted it was in her nature to lean on someone else and certainly not on a stranger. He guessed that tomorrow would be very different.

So, being Kelsey, he tried to marshal his arguments now. Though it was, he conceded, damned difficult to think at all with her warm body pressed to his side. He rested his cheek against her soft hair, scowling ferociously in an effort to stop thinking about that. And he was successful. Barely.

So. What would he say to her tomorrow? The pieces he had put together in talking to her still gave him very little in the way of a completed picture. He was certain that Meditron—meaning Blaine Mallory—was doing something shady, perhaps highly illegal, and very likely dangerous. He was also certain that Elizabeth's sister Jo was somehow involved; she was obviously being used as a lever to keep Elizabeth silent, but why? Had she somehow found out what was going on at Meditron?

Ami had definitely been the one to call the FBI;

he had recognized her voice immediately. And one thing that frightened young voice had said on the tape was branded in his mind: *They've got my sister.* Such a lost voice, desperate with fear and worry.

He didn't know how much Elizabeth knew, but did know that it would take time for her to trust him enough to talk about it. If they had that time. And if she didn't build new walls against him after what had happened between them in the kitchen.

What *had* happened between them? He thought he knew—but did she? Would she recognize the emotion he was increasingly certain of? Or would she, hounded by Mallory who, Kelsey thought, would hardly be subtle or gentle, decide that he was merely the lesser of two evils, the attraction purely physical with no demanding emotional issues?

"Damn," Kelsey murmured, rubbing his cheek half consciously against her soft hair. For a fleeting moment he wondered if Elizabeth had already given in at least partially to Mallory, and he felt something inside him knot painfully. No, no, of course she hadn't. She hadn't slept with the man. She wouldn't give in even physically to a man endangering her sister.

What about before? He tried to ignore the question, but it wouldn't go away. According to his research, Blaine Mallory had been in charge of Meditron for years, and he'd lived in Pinnacle all his life. Like Elizabeth. And she was so beautiful, *of course* the bastard would have tried. . . .

Kelsey wanted to break something. Mallory's neck, he decided, would fit the bill nicely. He wished he could laugh at himself for this unaccustomed savagery, but it didn't feel very amusing.

The very nature of his job had allowed little time for romance, no room at all for commitment, and precious little energy for either; he wasn't used to dealing with feelings like these. Even so, the thought of a rival had never disturbed him, even when one had existed. He had shrugged away desire and moved on, uninterested in fighting for what he wanted. And God knew he had never worried about a woman's past or possible lovers, rightly deciding it was none of his business.

And it wasn't his business now, except that he had the strong feeling that if he discovered Mallory was the kind of rotten scum who could sleep with a woman and then deliberately endanger and use her sister, he would quite certainly break the bastard into tiny pieces and scatter him to the winds.

"Is she asleep?" Ami had come out onto the porch, hovering uncertainly.

"Yes," Kelsey murmured, pulling his mind from violent thoughts and smiling a little.

Ami eased into a ladder-back rocking chair near the swing, and in the faint light from the living room window, her young face was serious. "She's tired. We had a rough winter; a late freeze damaged some of our peach trees, and that's worried her." Her voice was soft. "And, lately, Blaine's been pestering her. He's been after her since before she graduated from high school, but she never cared about him. But he's always coming around now, smiling and sweet-talking, those cold eyes of his looking at her until I want to hit him—"

"It's all right, Ami." More than all right, because she had told him something he needed badly to know. "I won't let him hurt Elizabeth anymore."

A tremulous smile curved Ami's lips. "Gosh, does it happen that fast? I mean—well, you *must* lo—care about her?"

Very conscious of the woman sleeping in his arms, he said softly, "Very much. So I guess it does happen that fast." And something in him shook on its foundations suddenly in a warning rumble that baffled him. He didn't know what it was, that feeling of foreboding, but his arm tightened around Elizabeth almost compulsively.

Ami tilted her head to one side. "But you want everyone to think you've known her for longer than a day?"

He pulled his mind back to the conversation. "That's very perceptive of you, little fawn. And quite right. So don't talk about it, all right? It'll be our secret."

Ami nodded and stood up, then looked a bit startled. "*What* was that you called me?"

"Little fawn."

"But why?"

"It's what you remind me of. A little fawn, shy and delicate, all legs and sometimes awkward. With big eyes and a face that'll break hearts someday."

Ami drew a deep breath. "Really? You aren't just saying that to be kind?"

He laughed almost soundlessly. "No, honey, not to be kind. You're growing so fast that your skin can't keep up with those lovely bones—but it'll catch up. And when those high school prom queens look into mirrors and realize all the beauty is behind them, you'll just be blooming."

Ami made an inarticulate little sound and rushed from the porch, surprising him.

Elizabeth raised her head and pulled gently away from him just then. "Thank you," she said quietly. "You convinced her when I've been unable to. She thinks she's ugly, and it's hard for her to believe she'll be lovely one day."

"Was she crying—?"

"Yes, but don't worry. You don't know it, but you just won yourself a devoted little sister." Elizabeth sighed softly, her gaze skittering away from his.

Steadily, Kelsey said, "No matter what happens between us, Ami has a friend in me as long as she needs me." And he wondered why he questioned a possible future when a large part of him was so very *sure*.

Although she hadn't slept very long, it seemed the nap had restored Elizabeth's balance somewhat. She gave him a very direct look. Both of them were clearly visible to the other in the light from the living room window. "Nothing is going to happen between us."

He hesitated, then said quietly, "Something already has, and we both know it."

Her lips firmed stubbornly., "No. You said yourself that you took advantage of—"

"That's how it began," he interrupted. "But it turned into something else. Elizabeth, I didn't come here planning on romance. And if I had a choice, I'd sure as hell pick another time, because when my business and romance clash, there's apt to be quite an explosion. But I don't have a choice. And I don't think you do either."

Elizabeth looked at the big, quiet man gazing at her so steadily, and felt her heart lurch. Oh, *damn*, how had this happened? Why couldn't she tell him with sure belief that it was his imagination, that of course there was nothing between them. That she would never think of getting involved in any way with a stranger, much less a stranger who had appeared abruptly in her life claiming that he wanted to help her? A stranger with heaven only knew what kind of past.

"Go away," she whispered.

"I can't."

She forced a shaky laugh. "Because it's your job."

"Partly. Because it's my job. Because your family is in trouble and I want to help. Because I held you in my arms and . . . I wanted you."

She felt an odd, warm shiver somewhere deep inside her, and a part of her recognized that this man, this stranger, possessed a kind of charm she had never before encountered. Charm and something else, something she *felt* to be honest, and yet frantically mistrusted. Something . . . caring.

He rose to his feet then, and pulled her gently up. "You need to think, I know," he said quietly. "Think about everything, Elizabeth, but one thing especially. *I can help you.* I swear to you, I can help."

"With your trusty sword?"

He smiled a little. "That, and a few other little tricks. I know you're afraid for your sister, afraid that if you do anything at all, tell anyone, it'll just be worse for her. But you're wrong. The most important thing to me is making sure she's safe as quickly as possible. Then I'll worry about what Meditron is up to. Do you understand that, Elizabeth?"

Inconsequentially, she said, "Everybody calls me Beth."

"I know."

She gazed up at him and, after a moment, nodded. "All right. I'll think about it."

He hesitated, then slipped his arms around her and drew her slowly toward him. "And think about this," he murmured as his head bent toward hers.

Elizabeth could have pulled away; he gave her the time and his hold on her was gentle. But she knew she wouldn't, even as her arms slid up around his neck, even as her body swayed toward his helplessly. She knew she wouldn't. And when his mouth covered hers, she felt more than heard the faint sound in the back of her throat.

And trapped somewhere in her mind was the incredulous thought that she was twenty-six years old and hardly unkissed; why had she never felt these feelings before?

She could feel her heart pounding through every square inch of her flesh, feel the blood rushing through her veins with a new heat. Her body was molding itself to his in an unconsciously seeking, hungry movement, the hard response of his body a strangely intimate shock that weakened her legs. And she could feel him moving against her now, subtle movements that inflamed all her senses and trapped yet another faint sound in the back of her throat.

His hair was like silk, she thought dimly, threading her fingers through it compulsively. And his body was so large and hard, his arms so strong as they held her. Her breasts were aching. She wanted him to touch them with his hands, his lips. She pressed even closer to him, no room left for shock at the wildness of what she was feeling.

Kelsey made a rough sound, his arms tightening, his lips slanting suddenly across hers to deepen the kiss. He was fast losing control and knew it, knew if he didn't stop this soon he wouldn't be able to. He hadn't been prepared for her instant response . . . or his own. Blindly, caught up in something beyond his experience, he kissed her as if that alone was an act of possession. And when his lips left hers at last with a wrenching effort, it was only so that he could explore the soft skin of her throat.

"Elizabeth," he muttered hoarsely, aching. The sound of his own voice, the sound of her name, helped him to regain some control over raging desire. This was not the time or the place, and his mind forced his body to remember that. Gradually, slowly, his embrace became less fierce, and he cradled the back of her head with one hand so that her face rested against the hollow of his neck.

She was boneless against him, trembling slightly, and he could feel her warm breath coming quickly against his skin. And he barely heard her quiet, husky voice over the pounding of his own heart.

"What are you . . . that you can do this to me?"

Kelsey pressed his lips briefly to her forehead, then rubbed his cheek against her hair. "What are you," he repeated roughly, "that you can do this to me?"

Elizabeth drew back slowly, looking up at him with eyes that were dazed and wondering. "I—I don't—"

He stopped her words with a gentle finger over her lips. "Just think about it, Elizabeth. Think about all of it." The last thing on earth he wanted was to leave her, but he had to. He turned away and moved slowly to the steps, then paused for a last long look at her. "I'll be back," he promised.

She stared after him for long moments, then went into the house, her steps guided by habit, not thought. She found Meg standing just inside, smiling derisively.

"Necking on the front porch—at your age! My, Beth, how very grown up of you!"

Elizabeth looked at her for a moment. "Have you done your homework?" she asked more or less by rote.

"I didn't have any. And it's Friday anyway. Beth, what's got into you? Or do we both know the answer to that?"

Elizabeth stiffened, and she had never felt the ten years between them more than at that moment. Very quietly, she said, "I can hardly control your language or manners when you're out of my sight, Meg, but you *will* remember both inside this house. In future, keep remarks like that to yourself."

Meg's eyes flashed. "So I'm in the wrong again? It's fine for you to criticize *my* boyfriends and look at them like they were dirt under your feet, but I'm not allowed to say a word when my prim big sister is out on the front porch practically laying down for some man she hardly knows—"

"*Meg!*" The worst of it was, Elizabeth reflected unhappily, she could hardly argue the point. And another voice saved her just then from having to respond.

"Why you rotten little cat!" Ami exploded, descending the remaining stairs to glare at Meg. "You're just furious because a really terrific man kissed Beth instead of you! Kelsey makes those *creatures* you hang out with look like the pathetic animals they are, and you know it. You can't stand it, can you, Meg? It drives you crazy. You only flirt with Blaine—who's old enough to be your *father*—because it's Beth he wants, and you wiggle around in front of his brother because you know she can't stand him."

"That's enough." Elizabeth had control of herself again. And when she looked at Meg's furious, white face, she regretted that Ami had been so frank. "Meg—"

But Meg had whirled away, rushing up the stairs and slamming her bedroom door violently.

"Sorry," Ami said gruffly. "I know you don't like for me to do that. But she makes me so mad."

"I know, sweetie." Elizabeth wanted to crawl into bed and pull the covers up over her head. She sighed, then smiled at her youngest sister. "Thank you for cleaning the kitchen. I should have thanked Meg."

Dryly, Ami said, "That's all right; she didn't do anything. I fed Lobo, too, and the horses." She looked at Elizabeth searchingly, then said, "I like Kelsey."

"I know you do."

"You—like him too, don't you?"

With absolutely no idea of how to answer that, Elizabeth found another smile somewhere. "I'm a little tired, sweetie, so I think I'll turn in early. You should too if you're going to ride Minnow over to Susan's house in the morning."

"Okay." Then, offhandedly, she asked, "Is Kelsey coming tomorrow?"

"I don't know. I'll lock up down here."

Ami nodded. "Good night, Beth."

" 'Night, honey."

Without thinking, Elizabeth checked doors and windows, let Lobo out for a last run and then went up to bed. She showered and changed for sleep in the same unthinking manner, and it was only when she lay between cool sheets that she could no longer avoid her thoughts and feelings.

Especially her feelings.

Why? Why had that stranger affected her so powerfully? She had never in her life lost control like that! Not like that. . . . She turned restlessly in the bed, stingingly aware of the heavy, aching tautness of her breasts, the dull ache somewhere near the pit of her belly. She remembered his hands on her, his lips against her skin, and the very memory prompted a hot flush she knew was very real.

She was just confused,' she tried to convince herself. Yes, confused, that was all. Blaine had been bombarding her for weeks now, and his practiced seduction had merely taught her senses, awakened them.

You didn't feel anything with him. Nothing at all.

It was true—unless she cared to count a certain revulsion. There had certainly been no positive response. Blaine had managed a few kisses and touched her often, yet her only emotions had been disgust and aversion, especially in recent days. And as for her senses, her body had remained unaffected by him. Coldly unaffected.

But Kelsey . . . *Kelsey.* Was that his first name of last? Who *was* he? What was he? Could she trust him as he wanted to be trusted? Did she dare?

He was so kind with Ami, so gentle and comforting, speaking to her as an equal and a friend. Blandly undisturbed by Meg's rudeness. Polite, but steel-strong with Blaine. And with her he'd been disconcertingly perceptive. Quietly insistent. Confident that he could help her. Sensitive of her weary state of mind. His strong arms so warm and comforting . . . then so passionate . . . so wildly passionate.

He seemed a dozen men. A dozen baffling, fascinating, charming men.

Dear heaven, what should she believe? Was he using her in order to find out about Meditron? *Could* a man be so convincing that his body shook with desire? Could he pretend such an intensity of feeling that it had hoarsened his voice and swelled his body against her?

Don't think about that, she told herself fiercely, aware that the mental images stirred her senses to life again. Don't *think* about it!

What should she do?

She was still going over it all in her mind when sleep tugged at her unexpectedly, and she gave in gratefully. But there was little comfort in her dreams, even though she was blessedly unaware that she tossed and turned all night while her subconscious and her body remembered.

Kelsey automatically checked his motel room, his mind only half on the procedure until he found the electronic bug poorly hidden in a lampshade. He looked at it for a moment, then turned on his television set, his professional instincts mildly disgusted by the poor placement of the listening device. Dumb, he thought, to put it so near the television set.

He stood thoughtfully for a moment, then checked the parking lot out front with wary eyes from behind a curtain before leaving his room quietly. He moved with the silence of a predatory animal along the concrete walkway and around the side to the row of rooms at right angles to the front. He knocked softly at one of the doors and waited.

The door opened a moment later, revealing a very large blond man with serenely expressionless dark eyes and a hard, handsome face. The man stepped back to allow Kelsey to enter the room, then closed the door behind him and went to stretch out lazily on the bed. "Room's clear," he said softly.

"Mine's not," Kelsey said in response, taking the chair by the window.

"I'm not surprised." The blond man looked faintly amused. "Two members of the local constabulary tossed it a couple of hours ago. You didn't leave anything in there to furrow their law-abiding brows, did you?"

"No." Kelsey stretched out his long legs and contemplated them somewhat grimly.

The blond man lit a cigarette, his hooded eyes watching his guest. "Then," he suggested mildly, "I assume you did something to catch their attention? They didn't search or bug my room, so we can take it they don't generally do things like that to their occasional visitors."

Kelsey lifted his gaze to the other's face. "You don't have to try and be so damned subtle, Derek. Just ask."

Derek smiled a little. "Okay. Whose nose did

you put out of joint while you were supposed to be unobtrusive?"

"Mallory's."

After a moment of silence during which he blew a smoke ring and studied it critically, Derek said in a placid voice, "I assume you had a reason."

"I thought so." Kelsey didn't elaborate; instead he said, "He was quick, I'll grant that. And now we know the local boys are definitely in his pocket. How'd they get into my room, by the way? The manager?"

"Nothing so obvious. They picked the lock. I happened to be near your room while they tossed it; they didn't say anything of value. Then one of them went to the office, where he checked the register. A 'routine check,' he told the manager."

Kelsey grunted. "The cops in that patrol car you distracted from me earlier probably got my tag number. And if they didn't, one of the others soon will. They'll find out everything matches."

Derek blew another smoke ring and contemplated it. "Um. Think our local boy might have national connections?"

"You mean intelligence connections? It doesn't have that feel, does it?"

"No. It feels like a case of local boy makes good and pleases the community by pouring money into his hometown. Got to know where that money's coming from, though. Whatever he's selling can't have a local market, I'd bet."

"I'd be willing to cover that bet." Kelsey looked even more grim. "He's playing some nasty games, too. That call the FBI got. I've found the girl. Fourteen, and worried sick."

"Her sister's missing?"

"Looks that way. And the setup's perfect for strong-arm pressure." Hardly aware that his voice had grown savage, and that Derek's eyes had narrowed slightly, Kelsey went on. "Four sisters living away from the town, orphaned years ago, and trying to make a go of it alone. The oldest not out of her twenties. Elizabeth doesn't dare ask for help because that bastard's threatening her, two younger sisters at home to take care of and one of them a rebel with more temper than sense."

"Elizabeth?"

"Conner. Ami's the one who called, and Meg's the troublemaker. Mallory showed up; Ami says he's been after Elizabeth since she left school, and now he's holding some threat to Jo over her head and trying seduction. One look, and you know he's a shark. He sure as hell didn't waste any time in having his boys check me out."

After a moment, Derek said softly, "You've found out a great deal, it seems."

Kelsey scowled at him. "I told you not to be subtle. I hate that."

Derek laughed almost soundlessly. "All right. Let me see if I understand the situation. You found—heaven only knows how—the girl who alerted us. You also found her older sister, Elizabeth, who seems to have knocked you pretty well off your feet. Aside from the fact that one of her sisters seems to be missing and possibly held as hostage against her good behavior, she's also being forced to cope with the dastardly attentions of Mallory, whom you would dearly love to throttle. Right so far?"

"Not throttle. Tear apart."

"Uh-huh. And because of these various and sundry things, your attention has shifted somewhat from Meditron. To be blunt, you don't give a damn what they're up to out there. Your priorities have changed. First, you intend to restore the missing sister to her family, thereby removing Mallory's lever against Elizabeth. Second, if at all possible disarranging Mallory's face somewhere along the way. And third, you want to find out what's going on at Meditron, so that you can hopefully lock Mallory away for the duration of his natural life."

"Anybody ever tell you that you talk real good?"

"Constantly. Is my summation fairly accurate?"

"On the nose."

"Um. You going to tell the boss all this?"

"Are you out of your mind?" Kelsey demanded with polite incredulity.

"It was just a thought. He signs the checks, after all."

Kelsey had a brief suggestion as to what Hagen could do with his paychecks which, after consideration, Derek observed to be anatomically impossible.

"So it is," Kelsey agreed. He stared at Derek.

Derek stared back.

"Well?"

Derek shrugged. "It's your show. Where do we start?"

Three

"Raven, my favorite partner and dear old friend, how are you?"

After a moment, her voice reached him mildly through the long distance connection. "Why, I'm fine, Kelsey. And you?"

"Top of my form, love, top of my form. How's Josh and that commando crew of his?"

"Flourishing." There might have been a trace of amusement in her voice, but for the most part it remained placid. "Rafferty and Sarah have a little boy, did you hear? His name's Patrick. Zach and Teddy are well and obviously happy. Lucas and Kyle are fine. And Josh and I are just dandy. It's spring in New York, and the Mets will do great this year if they can straighten out their pitching staff. Does that cover it?"

"Yes." He cleared his throat. "Um, Raven—"

"Spit it out, Kelsey." She was definitely amused now. "You never were much on small talk."

He sighed. "Uh-huh. Look, friend, I need a favor."

"You've got it."

"I haven't told you what it is yet!"

"Since when did that matter?"

Kelsey smiled a little. "All right. Thanks. What I really need at this point is information, and quickly. I need everything you can find on a town called Pinnacle, a company named Meditron, and a man named Blaine Mallory. All are connected."

"Anything in particular you're looking for?" Her voice was brisk and businesslike now.

"The usual stuff. Hints of shady dealings, more money than there should be, investigations on the state or federal level. You know the drill. I've done some basic research, but there are a few cloudy areas I didn't have time to probe; see what you can dig up. Oh, and I need the blueprints and a recent floor plan of Meditron, from the ground up."

"Got it." A bit dryly, she added, "Should I ask why you aren't going through official channels for this?"

Kelsey hesitated, then cleared his throat a bit uncomfortably. "Well, the boss won't expect me to check in for a while yet, and I'd rather not do so until I have to. If I use my clearance to get the information, he'll know about it. And, anyway, I haven't got anything solid to report, so—"

"Kelsey."

"What?"

"What is it you don't want Hagen to know?"

He sighed. "Hell. If you *must* know, old friend, I don't want him to find out he's done it again. He's gotten so paranoid about losing agents that he might just pull me if he finds out too soon. I can't risk that."

"What's her name?" The amusement had returned to Raven's voice, but it was warm now.

"Elizabeth Conner. I think Hagen's a warlock. I also think I'm not ready for this, not one bit."

"None of us ever are," she observed.

"No, I suppose not. Well . . ."

"I'll get the information for you, Kelsey. Do you object to Josh and the others knowing?"

"Hell, no. Turn Zach loose with his computers and see what he can uncover. Rafferty and Lucas might hear something from their intelligence contacts. And Lord knows Josh can move a mountain of bureaucratic red tape when he wants. I don't mind at all. But I'm on a tight schedule. There's a girl missing, and I have a very bad feeling about Meditron." He briskly rattled off a phone number and added, "You can reach me here; it's the number of Derek's hotel room."

"Outlaw Derek?" she murmured.

"The very same."

"Um. Tell him hello from me, and that I haven't forgotten England."

"What happened in England?"

"Ask Derek. I'll be in touch as soon as we have something."

"Right. And, Raven—thanks."

She made a rude sound and hung up.

Kelsey cradled the receiver and sat staring at Derek. "I didn't know you'd worked with Raven."

"Yes."

"She said hello, and to tell you that she hasn't forgotten England."

"She wouldn't have."

Kelsey frowned at the blond man still lying lazily on the bed blowing smoke rings. "Well?"

Derek made a "tisk" sound when a smoke ring emerged imperfectly, then looked at his partner. "It was one of those cases where our dear, benevolent boss kept too damn much to himself. Raven's contact, unknown to us, was a double agent. I tumbled to that just in time to get her out before he defected; he'd planned to take her with him as a nice prize for the other side."

"Ah." Kelsey reflected. "We should have let Josh strangle Hagen. I knew it at the time."

"You'll have to tell me that story one day."

"I will. In the meantime . . ."

"Yes. Tomorrow will be a long day."

When Elizabeth rose from bed early the next morning, she felt better, stronger, and half convinced that at least part of the preceding day had been a dream. She showered and dressed, and as she was standing before the mirror in her bathroom putting up her hair, she tried to fully convince herself it had indeed been a dream.

Because things like that didn't *happen* to people like her. Ordinary, rational, responsible people like her. Besides, women just weren't swept off their feet by large masculine strangers these days; it was an age of caution between the sexes for one thing, what with the confusion in roles and various other puzzlements. And for another thing, men with the ability to sweep a rational woman mindlessly off her sensible feet were hardly found on every street corner—in this or any age.

Elizabeth glared at her reflection, only then realizing that she was wearing a pretty green silk blouse and white shorts that were short indeed. "Dammit," she muttered.

She didn't need his help, of course. She didn't *want* his help. Even if he could help, which he couldn't. Trusty sword notwithstanding. Heaven knew the man looked capable of slaying dragons or anything else that came along, but some dragons were just too damned dangerous to mess with, especially when a dear hostage was hidden in his cave.

Elizabeth shook away a tremor of fear and went downstairs, reminding herself that she was taking the only course of action available to her. She was waiting, as patiently as she knew how, for this whole thing to be *over*. Blaine had so much power locally that if he couldn't resolve this quickly, no one else would be able to. And even if she *could* get an outsider in to help there was no way to move fast enough. With the guards and electronic security at Meditron, they would always have warning and time enough to . . . bury the evidence.

Oh, God, no, she prayed fervently.

She fixed a light breakfast for herself automatically, taking note of the signs that both her sisters had been before her. Ami would be at Susan's now, since they were practicing for an upcoming horse show, and Meg—as usual—would be with her friends in town.

Cleaning up after herself, Elizabeth found her thoughts turning again to Kelsey, and swore softly. It was all just so complicated! Who was he? *What* was he? Riding into her life in his beat-up car and making noises like her knight in shining armor. Dammit. That was garbage, that's what it was. Just garbage. Knights had died with Camelot.

The silence of the big house and her own muddled thoughts finally drove Elizabeth outside for fresh air and something to occupy her. She made her way to the barn and whistled for her horse, a big chestnut gelding the color of a vibrant sunset. Buddy willingly stuck his head into the light nylon bridle and stood patiently while she strapped a bareback pad on his broad back. She hardly needed the pad's strap for balance, but used it mostly for the sake of her white shorts. She swung aboard the horse, then bent and removed her sandals, setting them on a handy fence post near the road as they passed.

Elizabeth had wondered from time to time what kind of woman she would have become without the responsibilities of raising her sisters and keeping the peach orchard in business. She was not, she knew only too well, a sedate person at heart. Her control had become ingrained over the years, but sometimes her emotions went winging away from her, wild and uncontrollable, as if some deeply buried part of her knew they had to fly occasionally or else forget how to do it.

It happened no more than once or twice a year, a brief period when she felt the abandoned singing of her emotions, her senses. She had to fly, *had to*, and the next best thing to wings of her own was a fleet horse with racing Arab blood in his veins and the willingness to fly for her.

They went over the wooden pasture gate in an easy leap, crossing the driveway in one stride as Buddy settled down happily to run. Barely guiding him with her knees, Elizabeth leaned forward to silently urge him on as they raced along one of the wide lanes between the blooming peach trees. She felt her hair snatched by the wind of their

speed, aware that pins had scattered and that it
flew out behind her like a banner.

She didn't care. Faster and faster, pausing only
momentarily to turn a corner from one lane to the
next, they flew. Her heart was thundering, the
wind whistling in her ears, and she laughed aloud
with the glorious sense of freedom. Nothing troubled her for these brief, precious moments, no
problems, no dangers to heart or family. She was
not a woman who had been alone too long with
her responsibilities, but a soaring spirit refusing
to be caged long enough to forget how to fly.

Kelsey heard the hoofbeats before he saw her,
and he stood by his car in the driveway scanning
the orchard keenly. She was at first only a distant
flash of fiery red and green and white, the horse's
big body moving so swiftly the colors were only a
blur. But they were working their way back
toward the drive, and Kelsey felt his heart stop when
he could see her clearly.

Her spun-silver hair flowed out behind her, long
and shining in the morning sunlight. Her lovely
face was flushed from the wind, her long golden
legs seemingly a part of the horse's gleaming sides.
Horse and woman emerged from the surrounding
peach blossoms, the vital aliveness of summer
after the hazy dream of spring.

Kelsey had moved into the lane as they approached, and stood his ground while the horse
stopped with a head-swinging, sliding motion that
was curiously graceful. The big animal stood still,
snorting softly, flanks moving quickly, and Elizabeth looked down at Kelsey with something wild
in her eyes.

"One brief shining moment," she murmured huskily.

Kelsey stepped closer, resting a hand on the horse's shoulder as he looked up at her. "What?"

The wildness in her eyes refused to settle, like a falcon ignoring its handler's commands. "There was a place called Camelot," she said. "But it didn't live long. Like all dreams, it died too soon."

Kelsey reached up, his big hands encircling her waist easily as he drew her slowly from the horse. He kept his hands at her waist when she stood before him, and looked into the vivid, unhooded eyes of a soaring falcon. "The world remembers," he told her quietly, almost hypnotized by those eyes, very conscious that he was looking into the iridescent depths of an unguarded soul. And aware that she would not have chosen to let him see, not a stranger, not a man she didn't fully trust. But he saw, and was deeply grateful that he saw.

"Who are you?" she asked then.

"I'm the man who wants to help you," he told her.

She tilted her head a bit, vivid eyes questioning. "Why?"

"Because . . . it's important to me. Because I don't ever want you hurt again." He wondered, vaguely, what had happened to the bull about his job. Who cared? And he fiercely ignored another shudder from something inside him that was like an earthquake ripping through solid rock.

Her eyes were settling a bit now, finally but slowly. "But *who* are you?" she asked intensely. "What are you? I know your name, but I don't know who you are. And I have to know who you are, because—"

"Because?"

She shook her head a little, and the last of the wildness vanished into guarded depths. She looked at him then, really looked at him, and anger stirred. She removed her hands from his forearms and stiffened. "I don't know why you came back here. I can't help you."

Kelsey pondered for a moment, then said coolly, "I don't need your help."

She backed away from him warily. "No questions about Meditron or Blaine?"

"No. It isn't necessary. I can get the information I need from another source."

"Why did you come back here then?"

"I wanted to see you."

"Oh, right." She laughed softly, scornfully. "One look at me and this great passion was born?"

He smiled a little. "Something like that."

Elizabeth said something derisive, and it wasn't "malarkey." "I've heard that line too many times, pal; it had ivy growing on it when my grandmother was a girl. She didn't believe it, and I don't believe it. If you think I'm going to—"

"I think," he interrupted mildly, "that I'll be in your bed before the weekend's over." He caught her wrist easily before her hand could make contact with his face, holding it firmly. And holding her enraged eyes with his own, he added in the same blandly certain tone, "You know it as well as I do."

She jerked her hand away, her face white. "Bastard."

"I've been called worse." He wondered then which Elizabeth he would find in that bed. This one, he thought, this angry woman who would fight him every inch of the way—with perhaps a bit of the falcon thrown in. He didn't doubt that he would, sooner or later, end up in her bed; what was between them was just too damned explosive not to consume the both of them eventually. He only hoped that neither the falcon's wings nor his own suddenly vulnerable heart got singed in the blast.

"Get off my land!"

He sighed. "We've been through this, Elizabeth. I'm not leaving."

"I don't want you here, can't you get that through your head?"

Kelsey grinned suddenly, unable to help himself. "I think I got that, yeah. You made it very clear. It's a good thing I don't have a fragile ego."

"You have a *monumental* ego!"

He rubbed his chin thoughtfully. "Possibly. It's taken a few knocks, you understand, but I generally get what I want in the end."

With a curious, smothered sound that might have been a reluctant laugh, Elizabeth turned away and grasped her patient horse's reins. She snagged her sandals from the fence post as she passed, leading Buddy to the gate she hadn't bothered to open earlier. The bareback pad was unbuckled and left on the fence along with the bridle, and Buddy trotted away through the pasture to join another horse grazing near a barn in the distance.

Elizabeth put her sandals back on, looking up as Kelsey joined her to ask irritably, "Are you still here?"

"Certainly I'm still here," he said, wounded. "Faint heart never won fair lady, you know."

She gave him a baffled look and headed toward the house, with Kelsey following along behind.

"Did you," he wondered conversationally, "wear those shorts for you or for me?"

"Don't be ridiculous!" she snapped over her shoulder.

"I was just going to say that if you wore them for me, I certainly appreciate them," he explained apologetically.

Elizabeth bit her lip to contain her smile, glad he couldn't see and suddenly very conscious of his presence behind her. Oh, *damn* the man, why did he keep changing on her? Didn't he know she was so off balance now that anything— Know? Of course he knew!

Just inside the living room, she whirled and jabbed a finger into his chest. "It won't work!"

He had been continuing to admire the shorts, and looked up hastily. "What?" Pulling on his most innocent expression, he waited for her to explain.

"Your little game, that's what." She stared up at his face, ignoring his guileless expression. "You think I'm such an idiot that I can't figure it out? You could charm a snake, pal, but you aren't going to charm *me* into telling you anything."

"I'm not?"

She glared at him. "No, you're not!"

Kelsey tilted his head to one side and asked hopefully, "Can I seduce you into telling me something?"

"No, dammit!" She was trying desperately not to laugh.

"Well, hell, you haven't left me many options," he told her indignantly. "We federal agents only have so many methods to work with, you know. I mean, if you take away charm and seduction, how am I supposed to do my job?"

Elizabeth was biting her lip and gazing up at him with an unconsciously fascinated expression. She cleared her throat carefully. "I couldn't say."

"You know, you should leave it down all the time."

She blinked. "What?"

"Your hair. You should leave it down."

With an effort, she ignored the non sequitur. Evenly, she said, "I'm telling you to get the hell out of my life, understand? Get into your car and drive off my land. Stay away from my family. We don't need your help."

Kelsey looked at her for a moment, then stepped over to a chair and sat down on the thickly padded arm. He took due note of the increasing anger in her expressive face, but headed off whatever she was about to say by speaking in a calm and thoughtful voice. "I can see we have several problems here that need very badly to be resolved."

"Oh, you noticed that?"

"It was a little hard not to notice. First of all, you deny that anything is wrong here, despite the fact that your sister is missing."

"Jo's staying with an aunt," Elizabeth said flatly.

"You don't have an aunt."

She stiffened and her eyes flashed. "What did you say?"

He sighed. "I said, you don't have an aunt."

There was more than anger in her vivid eyes now, something like fury. Her voice shook a little. "And just where did you get that information?"

"It's amazing what information you can dig up if you know where to look. Pinnacle has a newspaper, Elizabeth, and like all newspapers it keeps back issues on microfilm. I looked up the accounts of your parents' deaths, and your court battle to keep what was left of your family together. According to those accounts, the judge was persuaded to let your sisters be put into your custody because there weren't any other relations. No aunts, no uncles, no cousins."

Elizabeth narrowed her eyes. "When did you look it up? Today's Saturday; the newspaper office is closed."

Kelsey rubbed his jaw, studying her. Then he sighed. "Place has a flimsy lock," he offered.

"You broke in?"

He winced. "Let's call it entry without the proper permission, shall we?"

She pressed her lips together, but said nothing.

Kelsey eyed her for a moment, then nodded, satisfied. "As I said, the first problem is that Mallory apparently has you convinced that if you just keep quiet, Jo will be fine. The third problem is that you trust me about as far as you can throw your horse. And the fourth problem is that you very obviously suspect I'd do just about anything—using you included—in order to get what I want."

Elizabeth remembered that first kiss in the kitchen and the shocking interlude on the porch last night, and lifted her chin. "Suspect? I *know* you would!" she snapped.

For the first time in his professional career, Kelsey was torn. He knew the most important thing was to get Jo back safe and sound; there was no doubt of that. But as important to him as a young girl's life was Elizabeth's opinion of him. And in the back of his mind in that alert place born years ago out of necessity, a clock was ticking away vital moments.

He sighed. "Elizabeth, sit down, please. We need to talk."

"We've already talked."

"No." Kelsey shook his head wryly. "We haven't. And now we have to, because there isn't much time."

Unwillingly impressed by the gravity of his face and his sober gray-blue eyes, Elizabeth moved to the couch and sat down. "What do you mean—not much time?"

Kelsey remained where he was, looking at her and wishing everything were different. She suspected his motives, and he couldn't blame her for that. Only time would teach her to trust him, and how much time did they have? And what would happen if the desire he could feel throbbing constantly throughout his body, a desire he knew she shared, caught them both before she learned to trust him? What would that do to them?

"Elizabeth . . ." He sighed roughly. "I don't want to scare you, but I've been in this business a long time, and I've seen a great many hostage situations. They're potentially explosive for many reasons. If a hostage knows who the captors are, there's always the possibility of testifying later in court. And if a hostage is held because of some information she has, she isn't going to just forget it. Not, at least, as far as her captor is concerned."

She stirred a little on the couch, staring at him with mistrust on her face but anxiety in her eyes.

Kelsey hurried on. "If Mallory's holding Jo only until he gets something done—gets the evidence out of the way of whatever he's doing—then maybe he will let her go, because then it would just be her word against his. But I don't *know* that. I can find out what's going on at Meditron, but without your help, I'm searching blindly, and Jo could get hurt because of that. If I push the wrong button because I don't have information I need, I could stampede Mallory, cause him to move too fast. Do you understand that?"

"Yes," she whispered through stiff lips.

"Then trust me," he asked softly.

"I don't know you." She hesitated, then blurted, "It's my sister's *life* we're talking about! How can I trust you with that?"

"How can you trust Mallory?" he countered.

She bit her lip. "I've known him all my life."

"He's a shark," Kelsey told her flatly.

Elizabeth almost smiled. "But a shark I know."

Kelsey half nodded to acknowledge the point. "As in 'better the devil you know than the one you don't'?"

"Yes."

He tried to ignore the inner sense of time rushing, and concentrated on this moment. Abruptly, without even realizing he was going to, he said, "My father was an agent. I remember I was sixteen when I found out; until then, I'd thought he was just a businessman. But that time, he came back from one of his "business" trips with his arm in a sling and a bullet hole in his shoulder. That's when I heard the *real* facts of life." He smiled a little.

Elizabeth was interested despite herself and felt oddly moved because there was something constrained in Kelsey's voice; this was not, she realized, something he had told many people. She waited quietly, hands folded in her lap, studying the face that had gone blank and hard after the smile died.

Another face. Another face he was showing her.

"For a few years we pretended everything was normal. My mother died and Dad threw himself into his work. I was in college, busy with my own life. Then I came home for summer vacation in my junior year, and Dad wasn't there. Weeks went by. I finally called the "emergency" number he'd given me. The next day, I got a visit from his boss, Hagen."

Kelsey was hardly aware that he had slipped back into the past, barely conscious that he was twisting the big signet ring around and around the third finger of his right hand.

"It was so unreal," he mused almost to himself. "If you could only see Hagen. He's a round little man with a cherub's face, a walking caricature of the self-important banty rooster. And this unreal little man was telling me that my father was on an unreal assignment, and they'd lost contact with him."

"What did you do?" Elizabeth asked softly.

He looked at her, his face still hard and remote. "I was twenty-one, reckless. I demanded that Hagen let me look for my father. He agreed; I've never known why. Anyway, he gave me the information I needed, swore me in as an agent, and three days later I found myself charming my way into an international smuggling ring."

When he said nothing more, Elizabeth said, "Kelsey?" very softly.

Kelsey, even with the remembered pain and bitterness tearing through him, heard her use his name—really use it—for the first time, and he was unaware of the longing in the look he gave her.

Inexplicably, she flushed, and asked him huskily, "What happened?"

"I enjoyed it," he said, face remote and voice bleak. "At first. It was exciting in a way I'd never known. And at twenty-one who thinks of dying? What kid ever thinks it can happen to him or to someone close to him?"

"Your father?"

Kelsey drew a deep breath and released it slowly, raggedly. "He'd infiltrated the ring just as I had, but he hadn't been so lucky; they found him out. Maybe he said the wrong word or gave someone a wrong look. Sometimes that's all it takes. Anyway, they decided to make an example of him days before I got there. And they were creative about it. We were aboard an old freighter on the open sea, and I hadn't been able to search the hold. I found out why when they brought . . . what was left of him up and threw him overboard."

"Oh, my God," Elizabeth whispered. She rose without thought and went to him, drawn as she would have been drawn to any wounded animal with anguished eyes. She placed one of her hands gently on his shoulder, and he took the other in both his, staring down at it blindly.

In a monotone, he went on. "I could see he was dead; nothing human could have lived like that. And the worst of it was that I couldn't react, couldn't let them see what I felt. There were thirty of them, and we were in the open sea. I wasn't armed. What could I do? I watched them throw my father overboard, and I turned as if it didn't matter to me and walked away. And I guess I was convincing, because they never suspected me. We made port a few days later, and Hagen had an army out there an hour after I called him."

"Kelsey, I'm sorry."

He was still holding her hand gently in both his, gazing down at it. "I went home. Back to college. I guess I even tried to act like a normal kid again. But I didn't fit anymore. I'd seen something I could hardly bear to live with, and it would be with me for the rest of my life. There were CIA recruiters at my college; when they offered me a job, I accepted. I worked for them about five years. Then Hagen came back into my life, and reminded me that he had sworn me in first and asked what the hell I was doing with the Company. He offered more freedom. I took it. And I fit in his world too.

"I think that, for a while, I got some kind of satisfaction out of defying death. I became a danger junkie. I just didn't give a damn what happened. I took the most insane chances."

Elizabeth found that she was softly kneading his shoulder, instinctively trying to ease taut muscles. Her eyes were burning and there was a lump in her throat.

Kelsey shook his head a little. "God knows what would have happened if I hadn't had the luck of the Irish and several outstanding partners over the years. My luck held long enough for those partners to straighten me out." He looked up at her then and forced a small smile. "I've been an agent almost fifteen years."

Elizabeth hadn't realized she was standing so close until he looked up at her. She was, she realized then, standing between his knees. Too close . . . too close. But she couldn't move away, couldn't break the hold of his slate gray eyes. She cleared her throat. "Why did you tell me?"

He shrugged. "You said you didn't know me.

Now you know more about me than most of the friends who've known me for fifteen years. Maybe that'll count for something." He sounded almost tired, and his face had the strained look of something held still for too long.

She didn't know what to think. Trust him—or not trust him? Which was the real Kelsey? This quiet man with pain in his eyes, or the one who would lightly charm and passionately seduce? Unaware of the confusion in her voice, she said, "I don't trust you, Kelsey."

"I know you don't. But I wish like hell you would."

"You confuse me. You say you want to help. But you also said that this weekend we would—"

"Be in your bed." He sighed softly. "I didn't count on this, Elizabeth. I didn't count on you. In my business, you don't get close to anyone involved in the situations you're investigating, because it puts you in danger. In danger of losing your objectivity. In danger of caring too much about the 'wrong' things. In danger of forgetting all the training and years of experience."

He released her hand, finding her waist and gently pulling her down until she was sitting on his thigh. His voice became lower, deeper, his eyes intent as they searched her face. "A good agent has to be virtually autonomous, able to act instantly and think only of resolving the situation. When you're . . . self-contained, nothing can hurt you. You do your job and walk away. But when you lose that autonomy, when there's someone involved who means too much to you, it makes the job harder. It makes you doubt yourself."

"I don't understand what you're telling me," she managed.

"I think you do. You're too much a woman not to."

Elizabeth was very conscious of his hard thigh beneath her, of the latent power of his arms, one around her back and the other lying still across her bare thighs. "I can't help wondering if you'll—"

"Walk away from this job when it's finished?"

She nodded mutely.

"No," he said, and felt again that inner shudder, that rumble of warning.

Shaken, Elizabeth protested, "How can you know? You said that you found your work exciting, dangerous. Once this job is done, there won't be any danger here, Kelsey. It's a small town in the back of beyond; there isn't anything here!"

"You're here."

Elizabeth swallowed hard, and she was only distantly aware that she was speaking at all. "You can't catch the wind," she whispered. "Chain the lightning. And you're as elusive as those elements. Somehow, I know that." *So many faces. So many men he had shown her.*

Kelsey understood what she was saying; the problem was that he wasn't entirely certain if she was wrong. Some rational part of his mind just didn't know for sure. *Would* he be content without the harried dangers of fifteen years? Could he step out of Hagen's world where he fit so well and into Elizabeth's where he might not fit at all?

His hesitation was telling. "I—I don't know, Elizabeth. I won't willingly walk away, I know that."

"What do you want from me?" she nearly wailed.

He hesitated again, torn between agent and man, wondering if there was, after fifteen years, any real boundary line between the two. "Trust me. Let me help you. Let me help Jo."

"And that's all?"

"You know it isn't."

Elizabeth tried to draw away from him, but stopped when his arms tightened. "It can't be both," she said tautly.

"It is both." He could feel his iron control slipping, and there was a raw sound to his voice. "Dammit, Elizabeth, I want you! I can't just turn that off."

Bewildered as much by her own feelings as by him, she let anger shape her words. "I imagine it's happened before in fifteen years, hasn't it? Autonomous or not, I'm sure there's been a little sexual tension here and there. We're both adults; why not call a spade a spade? Blaine has the same problem, I'm afraid. But at least *he* pretends to love me." She wasn't really sure, but she thought she heard Kelsey curse bitterly just before his lips captured hers.

And Elizabeth was bitter herself, furiously bitter, because her mind and body, for the first time in her adult life, seemed jaggedly separate. Confusion, mistrust, and anxiety were a jumble in her mind, but her body responded with instant flaming desire to his searing kiss. Her hands moved slowly up corded forearms, touched the short sleeves of his shirt, slid over the smooth material until she could feel the muscles padding his shoulders and back.

She was feeling with every sense, aware as if all the nerve endings of her body were sensitized by his touch. But, even more, she felt *his* feelings; with a powerful empathy she had never known before, she could *feel* his anger and his need, feel some terrible battle taking place inside him. And she had the strange, overpowering impression that Kelsey himself wasn't completely aware of that inner war, or that if he was aware, that he was fighting to ignore it.

His lips left hers finally to trail down her throat in a hot demand, and Elizabeth spoke huskily without even thinking about it. "No. You're angry."

"Yes, I'm angry," he said thickly against her throat. "I'm angry because I've got no business staying on this job. I should leave, let another agent take over. But I can't leave. You matter too much. Dammit, Elizabeth."

She was aching all over, fighting a mad desire to give in to the emotions storming through her with frightening force. But her mind could no longer control the separate entity that was her body, that hungering, splintered part of herself that wanted him beyond all else. Her fingers tangled in his thick hair and her head fell back, allowing him more room to explore, and the heat of his mouth on her flesh sent a wild tremor through her.

"Kelsey . . ."

He murmured wordlessly, a raw sound, and one big hand cupped the back of her head as he abandoned her throat to fit his mouth to hers again. He kissed her with a hard, driven passion, exploring her mouth, taking it fiercely. And when that devastating kiss ended, Elizabeth couldn't even reclaim the breath he had stolen from her.

"You belong to me," he said flatly, hoarsely.

She looked at his hard face through dazed eyes. "No," she whispered, distantly terrified of losing herself in the elusive complexity of this man. How could she belong to him when she didn't know who or what he was? How could she risk the most vulnerable part of herself by placing it in his keeping? No. She couldn't.

He held her eyes with his own, knowing he walked a knife's edge, knowing he was moving too fast. But he had no choice. There was no time, no time for the patience and rituals of courtship. "You belong to me," he repeated. "You know it, and I know it. Say it, Elizabeth. Admit it."

She swallowed hard, caught in the slate gray of his eyes. She was confused, aching, frightened by the intensity of his demand and by her own instinctive urge to admit what he demanded. "I . . . No, I can't . . . I won't."

"You have to," he said ruthlessly, driven by the impersonal ticking of his inner clock. "Stop thinking, Elizabeth, and *feel*. Your body knows you belong to me. Do you want me to prove it? If I carry you up those stairs, will you be able to say no?"

She closed her eyes, a ragged sigh escaping her. "Damn you. Oh, damn you."

Four

The admission, dragged from her totally against her will, was too devastating to let stand alone and vulnerable, and Kelsey knew it. Quietly, he said, "Feel me shaking, Elizabeth. Feel what you do to me. There hasn't been a moment since we met that I haven't been on fire with wanting you."

She looked at her fingers, still tangled in his thick hair, and forced her hands to move downward. But they would only move as far as his shoulders where they rested, feeling the hard padding of muscle over bone. And she could feel his hands, one still at her waist and the other at the back of her head, gentle fingers moving in her hair almost compulsively. She could indeed feel him tremble.

"It's just physical," she said finally, almost inaudibly.

The muscles in his jaws tightened, but his voice remained quiet. "Is it? Whatever it is, it isn't going to go away."

Elizabeth had never felt so torn. She wanted the man and mistrusted the agent—if that was what he really was. And, whatever he was, he had made her no promises, nothing she could hang on to. Was he using her to get information? Whatever his body felt, was his mind coldly calculating, probing the strength of her resistance? Why else would he have forced her to admit she couldn't say no to his desire?

She didn't know what to do!

In the same still, quiet voice, he said, "I could carry you up those stairs, Elizabeth. I could make you mine so completely you'd never doubt it again. We both know that. But you'd hate me for it, and fight me all the way. Not physically, but emotionally. I don't want that."

"You want information," she said dully.

Kelsey hesitated, then swore softly. "Yes, I do. But that's apart from us, apart from what we feel."

"No, it isn't."

"Elizabeth—"

"I'll tell you." She broke away from him with an abruptness that caught him off guard, moving to a window on shaking legs and staring out blindly. Would she be putting Jo into even greater danger? She didn't know, couldn't know. But she did know that she could no longer bear being torn by the question of whether Kelsey was bent on seduction simply to get the information from her.

She had to know!

Several hundred miles away in a high-rise office building in Manhattan, the weekend quiet of a certain floor was broken by Zachary Steele's disgusted voice.

"That's it. Far as I can take it."

Of the several people quietly watching his labors on the computer, only Raven spoke up. "And?"

"And nothing." Zach sat back, looking at the others thoughtfully. "I just ran head-on into a military code lock."

Josh Long, sitting close beside Raven on a vacant desk, frowned at his security and electronics expert, and friend of more than fifteen years. "Military? Now, that's a bit . . . unexpected, isn't it?"

Raven looked at her husband, worried. "What on earth has Kelsey stumbled into?"

Lucas Kendrick, chief investigator for Long Enterprises, turned away from another computer and shook his head at their inquiring looks. "No dice. Blaine Mallory's so clean he squeaks. Personal bills paid off or current, business accounts up to date. An A1 credit rating, and a pillar of his community. The IRS has no complaints with his returns, and if he's living above his income, he's hiding it very well. He hasn't put a foot wrong. Not even a traffic ticket."

Kyle, who was sitting on a low counter beside Luc's computer, looked baffled. "I don't get it. Mallory comes up clean, Meditron is protected by a military code lock, and Pinnacle turns out to be a nice little Southern town. What gives?"

Teddy, assuming her usual position in Zach's lap, said definitely, "Something fishy. Zach, why *would* the military restrict access to information on Meditron?"

"Only one reason I can think of. If Meditron's under contract to produce something for them they'd rather not let the public know about, they'd lock the data away and restrict access. Given the time, I could probably get access without asking, but if I trip one of their hidden security alarms, they'll know somebody's in their system."

Josh shook his head a little. "We've a good relationship with the military to date; I'd rather not annoy them. I can call General Ramsey and find out what he knows. Maybe he'll give me the access codes."

Rafferty Lewis came into the computer room just then with his wife, Sarah. Both looked troubled.

"You couldn't get it," Raven said.

"No." Rafferty glanced at the others, seeing no surprise. "I gather you've all had the same problem? If a floor plan for Meditron exists at all, nobody's talking about it."

Raven sighed. "Figures."

Sarah, Rafferty's wife, gazed around at the thoughtful faces and said, "Nothing at all?"

Zach shook his head. "Damned little. On the surface, there's some tame information about Meditron—all of it neat, clean, and apparently aboveboard. When I dug deeper, I found a military code lock."

Sarah glanced at Raven. "And Kelsey doesn't want Hagen to know about this?"

"No. He was definite—if a bit incoherent—about that."

"I'd give a lot to see Kelsey in love," Rafferty murmured a bit wistfully. "It really ought to be something to watch."

"You might get a chance," Josh said in an absent tone.

Zach looked at him for a moment, then said

mildly, "We can't all go tearing down there, no matter what we find out. It's a small town."

"Granted." Josh studied his companions one by one, his rather hard blue eyes considering. "First, I'll call the general and see what I can pry out of him. We can't decide much until we have something more to go on."

"It's commando time," Teddy murmured.

"They can't stand it," Raven agreed dryly.

Josh lifted an eyebrow at his wife. "We can't stand it? You know very well that you're wild to get down there and see what Kelsey's involved in."

Raven smiled innocently. "Who, me?"

She wasn't fooling anyone at all.

Kelsey had gambled, and he wasn't entirely certain if he had won or lost. He slipped down into the chair and watched her as she stood by the window, afraid to ask. His body ached incessantly, every muscle tense with control, and he had to clear his throat before he could speak.

"All right. Tell me."

Elizabeth drew a breath visibly, and her voice was even when she began talking. "Jo works at Meditron as a secretary. Blaine's secretary, as a matter of fact. Two weeks ago, she was scheduled to take a vacation; she was going to drive down to Florida. Her last day before the vacation she was late coming home. I got worried and called Blaine. He seemed . . . surprised. He said he'd check and get back to me."

"And?"

"About an hour later, Blaine came here. He was very upset, very angry. I've never seen him that angry. He said there were things I couldn't know, things he couldn't tell me, but that Jo had landed herself in a first class mess. He said that she was being held—to make *him* behave."

"What?" Kelsey's eyes narrowed. "You believe that?"

"I don't know what to believe." She didn't look at him. "But until two weeks ago, I would have sworn Blaine would never deliberately hurt anyone. You didn't see him that night. He was pale, angry, and . . . Somehow, I got the feeling he was very shaken. He said there was nothing he could do because of—of more than a threat to Jo. But he said she was safe, that they wouldn't dare hurt her."

"They?"

Elizabeth turned away from the window finally, crossing the room and sitting down on the couch. She was pale, strained. "I don't know who *they* are; Blaine wouldn't say. What he did say was that it would only be a couple of weeks, maybe a little more. He said that the security force at Meditron was no longer under his control, and that there was no way to get in there and get to Jo without alerting *them*. But they're treating her well. He sees her every day, and—"

"How do you know that?"

"He told me," she said stiffly. "He made them agree to that, he said. He lets me know how Jo is every day."

"Dammit," Kelsey muttered.

Elizabeth lifted her chin, her green eyes stormy. "I've known him all my life; he wouldn't lie to me about Jo."

Kelsey looked at her for a long, steady moment,

then said quietly, "You have to be honest with me now, Elizabeth. I want your instant reaction—from the gut, not the head. All right?"

She nodded a little uncertainly, puzzled.

He mentally gathered his questions, then began asking them in an impersonal, unthreatening tone. "Is Mallory an honest man?"

"Yes." She looked surprised, then thoughtful.

"Gut response?" he asked.

She nodded slowly.

"All right. Is he worried about Jo?"

"Yes. But . . ."

"But satisfied that she's safe for the time being?"

"Yes."

"Before two weeks ago, was Jo suspicious of something at Meditron?"

"Yes."

"What did she say?"

"That there was more going on there than people in town knew about. Something dangerous."

"Involving Mallory?"

"Yes. No." Elizabeth frowned.

"What was Jo's reaction, Elizabeth? Think. What did she say? How did she feel?"

"She seemed a little . . . well, disgusted at first. She said that Blaine had no business agreeing to such a thing, even if it was good for the town's economy. Then she suddenly became quiet about that; something else seemed to be bothering her. She said something about the guards at the gate being different, and that Blaine was mad as hell."

"About what?"

Elizabeth sighed, impatient with herself. "I don't think she ever said. Just that Blaine was mad, and that he'd said something about taking the matter to the top if he had to. That was the day before she disappeared."

Kelsey was frowning. "Let me get this straight. We're talking about two different things here. Mallory had 'agreed' to something that was helping the town; maybe it was dangerous, but Jo didn't have a major reaction to it. But then something else happened, something that made him angry, and bothered her a great deal more. That's your feeling about it?"

"Yes," she said slowly, realizing the separate occurrences for the first time.

"How long had Jo worked for him?"

"About two years. But I remember now how upset she was when Blaine finally told her what he'd agreed to. She kept after him; she's like that. There's a part of the plant townspeople don't work in, just outsiders, and she asked him what had been going on there—apparently for several years."

Absently, Kelsey said, "It'd have to be at least a few years; money's been coming into the town's economy that long." He stared at her for a moment, then muttered, "Dammit, I wanted to clean his clock."

She blinked. "Blaine's?"

"Yes."

Elizabeth thought about that for a few moments, deciding not to attribute Kelsey's reaction to jealousy. That would be ridiculous, of course. "Then you don't think he's the one holding Jo, after all?"

Kelsey sighed. "My gut says no. Still . . . If I only knew what it was he agreed to, and who he made the deal with." He glanced at the telephone beside his chair and reached for the receiver, punching out a number quickly. He didn't say hello, just, "Anything?" And, after a moment, "Okay. Let me know." And hung up the receiver.

"Who did you call?" she asked.

"My partner."

For some reason she didn't question, the information reassured her about his identity as an agent. "I thought you were alone here."

"No. We came into town separately, and no one's tied us together; I'd like to keep it that way, at least for the time being."

Elizabeth was silent for a while, watching him as he sat frowning. Then, a little hesitantly, she said, "We could ask Blaine—"

"No. He *could* be just an unwilling pawn in whatever's going on, but I'd rather have a clearer view of the situation before I take the chance of tackling him with it." Kelsey brooded for a moment. "Take it to the top. The top of what? Who does he answer to, and what's stopping him now? Is it because they have Jo? And who the hell are they?"

"How can we find that out without asking Blaine or endangering Jo?" she asked him.

He sighed. "My partner's waiting for a call now from our source. With any luck at all, we'll have more information before the weekend's over. Until we know more, we can't take the chance of doing anything."

Elizabeth nodded, unconsciously bracing herself before she could utter her next words. "I see. Well, you know everything I do now. There's nothing else I can tell you."

Kelsey looked at her for a moment, then laced his fingers together over his flat stomach and stretched his legs out before him, presenting the appearance of a man making himself comfortable. "I guess not," he agreed mildly.

She linked her fingers together nervously. "You'll want to get back to your partner."

"He knows where I am."

"You can't stay here," she said tightly.

"Why not?"

"You got what you came here for."

"Not quite."

She bit her lip, trying to ignore the heavy ache of her body. Dear heaven, what had this man done to her? Why did she feel like this just because he was looking at her? "I've told you all I know. Now leave!"

He sighed a little. "Yeah, that's what I thought. Why is it so hard for you to believe I want you, Elizabeth? You thought I'd just walk out of here, didn't you? You thought I'd get the information and leave."

"You will."

"I wish it were that easy." His smile was crooked. "If I only had Meditron, Jo, and Mallory to worry about, everything would be relatively simple. Just another assignment, a tangle of threads to straighten out."

"It is that simple."

"You know it isn't." He didn't move, but his voice deepened and his eyes darkened like storm clouds; intensity came off him suddenly in waves, and she could clearly see for the first time the strength and danger of this man.

Elizabeth wasn't frightened, but she was instantly aware that something in her responded to his strength. That wildness inside her, the part that longed to fly. And why Kelsey? Why was that part of her so attracted to his danger?

Another face. Another man. Who was he?

"It isn't that simple," he was saying in that dark, still voice. "Do you know what an effort it takes to force myself to just *think* when I'm looking at you?"

She was trying to be rational, reasonable, even though her instincts told her it was hopeless. "We met barely twenty-four hours ago. That isn't enough time."

"How much time is enough? A week? A year? Elizabeth, I didn't need twenty-four hours to know I wanted you. Why is that so hard for you to believe?"

"You're not safe." She had spoken without thinking, responding to his stillness rather than his question. And even though some part of her was relieved that he apparently still wanted her, that her information hadn't changed that, she was afraid to give in to what could destroy her.

A frown creased his brow, and dark eyes darkened even more. "Are you afraid of me?" He sounded incredulous.

Elizabeth swallowed hard, and this time she knew what she was saying. "Look around you, Kelsey. Look at this house, this farm. It's a simple life. Do you know how long it's been since there was a murder in this county? There's no record of one, ever. The last robbery was five years ago; a bunch of kids raided Darcy Pemberton's peach shed, and then tried to sell his own crop back to him."

"Elizabeth—"

She went on as if she hadn't heard, her voice

quiet and reflective. "Most of the people in Pinnacle are fourth or fifth generation; their parents were born here, their kids will raise kids here. Maybe we have one of the last bastions of Small Town America; I don't know. What I do know is that for twenty-six years this has been my home. I don't know anything else."

"And I don't fit here; is that what you're telling me?" There was an echo of old pain in his voice.

In a sudden flash of intuition based on all the faces he had shown her, she said, "I think you'd fit wherever you wanted to." She looked at him, trying to bring the man into focus. But the flash was gone, and she shook her head a little. "What I'm telling you is that this is my life. And it'll be my life after you're gone. And what I'm asking you is please not to do anything to make *me* not fit anymore."

Kelsey didn't want to hear it; he really didn't want to hear. But he had to. "What do you mean?" he asked neutrally.

"You know what I mean." Her voice was almost inaudible. She looked fixedly at her fingers. "You're the mysterious stranger in town, and the heroine always falls for him. In the end, he always leaves her with a scrapbook full of memories. And she spends the rest of her tame life remembering that . . . that interlude of abandon." She lifted her chin, staring at him squarely. "I don't want that."

After a moment, he said in a hard voice, "You want guarantees. Happily ever after, and a white picket fence." Something moved inside him again, slowly, shuddering.

"No, not from you." She was looking down at her fingers again, and didn't see him wince. "I don't want anything from you, Kelsey. I don't want you to turn my life upside down. I don't want you to leave me with a memory of feelings too violent for my . . . my tame life. I don't want you to change me so that I won't fit here anymore."

She heard a faint sound and stiffened, but continued to look fixedly at her fingers. And it was a long time before she could bring herself to look up.

He was gone.

Elizabeth got through the remainder of the day simply by functioning on automatic. But while she went about her daily chores, the routine of keeping the family home and business operating, her emotions were in turmoil and her mind uncertain—to say the least. She told herself over and over that Kelsey's leaving was for the best, that she really *didn't* want him to teach her to feel things she could never feel without him, to become addicted to wildness.

Because where would that leave her? Dissatisfied with the life she had to live? Longing for feelings that were, in all probability, the result of a set of once-in-a-lifetime circumstances: Her tension and anxiety over her missing sister; the sudden appearance of an elusive, charismatic stranger; the equally sudden emergence of her rare feelings of wildness?

It was, she thought vaguely, like the links of a chain. Remove one link, and the chain no longer held. When he left . . . when Jo was safe and worry a thing of the past . . . when her burst of impetuous emotions had settled, as it always did

. . . Then her life, her sedate life, would be the same again. And what would it do to her future to have that memory of overwhelming feelings tormenting her?

Elizabeth had moved outside to the porch swing, and when she saw a car turn into the driveway she felt her heart thud in a suddenly uneven rhythm. Then she recognized the car, and if anything had been needed to convince her that Blaine could never stir her blood or touch her heart, she would have known then. She watched him get out of the racy silver sports car, noting with detachment that he was an extremely handsome man, that he moved with a panther's fluid grace. That he was, in some indefinable way, possibly as dangerous as Kelsey. A powerful man.

She felt nothing.

Blaine stepped up onto the porch and, when she didn't move from the center of the swing, sat down in a ladder-back rocking chair nearby. "Beth, who is this Kelsey?" he demanded flatly.

"Have you seen Jo?"

"Yes. She's fine. Beth—"

"It's been two weeks."

He looked at her for a moment, a long, lean, dangerous man, and his face was unreadable. "I know. And I'm sorry; I thought the whole thing would certainly be over by now. Just a few more days."

"And?" She looked at him steadily. "And what, Blaine? My sister has been held against her will; do you really think we're all just going to forget that?"

He sighed. "It's complicated."

"I'm not an idiot."

For the first time in quite a while, Blaine smiled, and his rather cold eyes warmed. "You're too damned smart for your own good. All you girls are."

"Who's holding Jo?"

"I can't tell you that."

"Why not?"

"I just can't. You'll have to trust me, Beth."

After a moment of silence, Elizabeth discovered that she understood this man, at least she understood him far better than before. Blaine asked for trust while offering none, and that told her much about his supposed feelings for her.

"Don't look at me like that," he told her irritably.

"Like what?"

He hesitated, then said, "My sister looked at me like that sometimes when we were growing up. It made me feel like she knew I'd just been sneaking a cigarette behind the barn."

Elizabeth smiled faintly. Then, with a sigh, she said, "You got into the habit of loving me, Blaine. But that's all it ever was. Just a habit."

"The hell it was!" His face was hard, his mouth a grim slash. "You're just upset because of Jo, but when all this is over you'll feel differently."

"No. I won't. Do you really think I could ever love a man who didn't trust me?"

It stopped him, but only for a moment. "That isn't it at all. I *can't* tell you anything."

She shook her head a little. "Won't, not can't. But it doesn't matter. I don't love you, Blaine. I won't marry you."

He was very still, his eyes cold again. "It's him, isn't it? That damned Kelsey. Who is he, Beth?"

Gently, she said, "That's none of your business."

Blaine got to his feet, his entire body stiff. "I'll make it my business," he said tightly, and turned away.

Elizabeth waited until he reached the steps, then said, "Blaine?"

He halted, looking back at her over his shoulder.

Her soft voice was underlaid with steel. "If something should happen to Kelsey, I'll know where to look."

He went white. "You think I'm capable of that?"

"I think you're capable of just about anything." She sat in the swing, idly moving it back and forth, and watched him drive away in a cloud of dust. And slowly, very, very slowly, she began to get angry.

Kelsey nearly stumbled over a large vacuum cleaner just inside the doorway of Derek's room, and growled, "What the hell is that?"

"Now, what does it look like?"

"I'm not in the mood for games, Derek."

The big blond man looked at his partner for a moment, then said softly, "No, I see you're not. That, my friend, is a vacuum cleaner. It's also my cover. I'm a salesman, remember?"

Kelsey grunted and lowered himself into the chair by the window, reaching into a paper bag he carried and producing a bottle. "Damned county's dry," he muttered. "I had to drive fifteen miles to get this." He didn't bother with a glass. Staring moodily at the vacuum, he asked, "Sell any of those?"

"Three, so far."

"Any word from Raven?"

"No."

Kelsey looked up to intercept a very thoughtful look from his partner, and warned, "Don't lecture me."

"I wouldn't think of it," Derek said politely. He sat down on his bed and reached for a package of cigarettes, saying in a mild tone, "One of my customers this morning happened to mention that she'd noticed several military uniforms out at Meditron when she picked her husband up one day."

Kelsey, his training and experience too deep to be much influenced by his black mood, frowned and briefly related what Elizabeth had told him a couple of hours earlier.

Derek listened thoughtfully and said, "Think Mallory might have made his deal with the military?"

"Unless your customer confused security uniforms with military ones, it sounds like a good bet."

"Unlikely. She's an army brat."

Kelsey nodded, his moody gaze returning to the bottle he held. "I don't have much use for the military, but I can't see them holding a twenty-three-year-old woman hostage."

"A renegade, maybe?"

"Hell, who knows? From what Elizabeth said, it seems Mallory was furious and planning on taking the matter to the top. If some renegade soldier in charge of their doings at Meditron was going farther than Mallory had agreed to . . . If that soldier was acting on his own authority with whatever it is . . . If Mallory threatened him openly, and he decided to get himself some leverage in the shape of Jo . . . Hell. Too many ifs. Too damned many ifs. We're working in the dark."

"Are you going to drink all of that?"

"I told you not to lecture me."

"Who's lecturing? I just asked a question."

"Worried about your hide, partner? Don't. I'll come through when it counts, professional all the way."

After a moment, Derek said quietly, "Low blow, friend."

Kelsey swore, capped the bottle, and tossed it over to lie on the bed. "Yeah. Sorry. I can't seem to keep my foot out of my mouth today."

"Getting a little hard to see the boundaries?"

"Between professional and personal?" Kelsey shook his head. "Hard doesn't cover it, friend. I lost sight of those boundaries long ago. If they ever existed." He sighed roughly. "I've got to call Hagen."

"We have nothing concrete to report."

"Not that. Me. He's got to replace me. I'm a drawback on this assignment, maybe even an active danger." Kelsey's voice was hard, remote.

Derek studied him from hooded eyes. "I see. She really got to you, didn't she?"

Kelsey wasn't a man who confided easily in others. And what could he have said, anyway? That he was just barely able to function around Elizabeth, that he couldn't keep his eyes off her or his hands to himself? That he was desperately afraid she was right to fear his intrusion into her life, and that something inside him was shaking under a threat he had never felt before? That he wanted her until it required a wrenching physical effort to fight it, until he could only just manage to force himself to think and act professionally?

"She got to me," he said.

"You've been fifteen years in this business," Derek said. "You won't lose that."

"I am losing it. My instincts are colored by her. How can I be sure now? How do I know if a possibility *feels* right, or if I just want it to for her sake?"

"I'll risk it."

Kelsey shook his head. "I can't."

"Give it another day," Derek urged quietly. "You know damn well you'll go crazy if you pull out now, wondering what's happening, if she and her sisters are all right. Give yourself a little time away from her. We'll check out Meditron tonight, see if we can get close enough to find out what's going on."

Kelsey hesitated, but he knew his partner was right. He *would* go crazy, not knowing. "All right," he said finally, heavily. "But for God's sake, keep an eye on me; make sure I don't do something stupid!"

"Gotcha," Derek murmured.

When his partner had left to try and get a few hours' sleep before their planned postmidnight activities, Derek stretched out on the bed and lit a cigarette, frowning. No one had ever accused him of being either cautious or particularly concerned about possible dangers; the sobriquet of "Outlaw Derek" was one he was fully aware of, and often amused by.

He had earned that name with a long series of

seemingly reckless actions, and it was for that reason that he understood Kelsey very well even though they'd never worked together before.

His understanding was also due to Raven.

Happily married now and ostensibly out of the business, Raven nonetheless kept an unobtrusive but concerned eye on her ex-partner. She had somehow—Derek hadn't asked how—learned that he would be working with Kelsey, and had quietly arranged a brief meeting. Raven didn't tell tales out of school, but she had worked with Kelsey longer than anyone else, and she had explained a few things to Derek.

And, since one's life often depended upon understanding and trust of one's partner, and since Derek wasn't quite so reckless as he seemed, he had listened carefully.

Derek was troubled now, but not because Kelsey doubted his own instincts. He was troubled by something Raven had told him. *"He's a chameleon, Derek, and a totally unconscious one. He'll fit himself into any situation instantly without even thinking about it. The problem is, the real Kelsey has a hell of a lot of bitterness and pain trapped under all those roles. And one day, it's going to come out."*

Derek knew the reasons, as well as they could be known. He knew about Kelsey's father, and about others lost in fifteen years of a dangerous business. And today, he had for the first time caught a glimpse of that darkness in Kelsey. The man was torn, hurting, and something between him and Elizabeth Conner had intensified that pain.

It wasn't Derek's business, God knew, except

that it obviously affected this assignment. And since he liked Kelsey, he wasn't at all willing to stand by silently and watch the man tear himself apart if there was any way of stopping it.

But, was there anything he could do?

They were short on time and long on problems, and if Elizabeth Conner was the average, intelligent woman, she wouldn't trust Kelsey very far; she had every right to be wary about the entire business.

Derek hesitated, debated silently for a moment, then sighed and reached for the phone.

"Any luck?" Kelsey kept his voice low as he reached his partner; they had both spent the past hour slowly moving around the fenced perimeter of Meditron, taking care to stay out of range of the cameras.

Derek, dressed like Kelsey in dark clothing, shook his head. "Nothing. They work three shifts; all the buildings are lighted. There's no way to tell from out here if any one building is holding something it shouldn't."

They stood in the shadows of trees which completely encircled the fenced compound; there were some thirty feet between the trees and the fence all the way around the perimeter. There were several floodlights placed strategically about the six buildings, numerous cars in the parking lots, and the usual industrial noise escaping whenever a door was opened.

A normal industrial plant to all appearances. Except that security was unusually heavy, in the form of an electrified fence, perimeter cameras, two pairs of very alert patrolling guards complete with leashed and very alert dogs, and three armed guards standing watch inside what looked very much like a bullet-proof gatehouse.

"I think—" Kelsey began, then broke off abruptly as he felt a sudden itch between his shoulder blades. He had come to respect and pay attention to that sensation over the years, since it usually heralded trouble.

"Over there," Derek murmured, pointing toward a point in the trees about fifty yards away from them. "We've got company."

"I'll go."

"Yes," Derek said. "I think you'd better."

Alerted by something in that mild voice, Kelsey looked harder at the distant movement, then swore violently and vanished into the trees.

Derek made himself comfortable on the ground, leaning back against the trunk of a tree and thoughtfully studying Meditron. But his mind wandered a bit.

It seemed that Kelsey wouldn't find it easy after all to get some time away from Elizabeth Conner.

Not if the lady had anything to say about it.

Five

"What the *hell* are you doing here?"

Elizabeth nearly jumped out of her skin, even though the furious demand was whispered. She was dragged quickly back into the trees before she could respond, and even though the iron grip on her arm wasn't especially painful, she struggled. "Let go of me!" she whispered fiercely.

"No!" he snapped softly, continuing to drag her unwilling body until they were almost at the main road. His battered car was parked in the shelter of the trees, and he opened the back door and pushed her unceremoniously inside, climbing in after her too quickly for her to escape.

Elizabeth had taken just about all she was going to take. Her anger had grown all day, until she had finally decided she would be out of her mind if she just sat around any longer and waited for either Blaine or Kelsey to do something to free her sister. Until she had reached Meditron and seen the formidable barriers she would have to cross, she had not fully realized the imprudence of her action; she had simply acted because she had grown very tired of doing nothing.

Now she stared at Kelsey in the dimness of the car's interior and felt like a fool. It just made her madder. "Let go of me!" she whispered fiercely again.

Kelsey cursed violently. "Do you have any idea how close you came to getting yourself electrocuted—if not shot?" His voice was hard and hoarse.

She went still, and swallowed with difficulty. "I wouldn't have touched the fence; I saw the signs."

"What did you plan to do? Walk up to the gate and demand to see your sister?"

"I don't know!" She began struggling again. "Damn you, I just wanted to *do* something! You and Blaine just talk and talk—neither of you will do anything—and Jo's being held in there somewhere."

"I'm trying to do something," Kelsey told her harshly. "Dammit, Elizabeth, let me do my job!"

"It isn't a job to me!" she cried softly. "It's my sister!"

He tried to get a grip on his temper. "I know," he said in a quieter voice. "I know that. But you have to give us time and plenty of room to work."

She laughed, the sound almost a sob. "You? The Lone Ranger? Where's Tonto?"

"Back there keeping an eye on the place," he growled.

"And waiting! I'm tired of waiting, tired of expecting somebody to do something! *I'm* somebody! Dammit, let go of my arm."

Kelsey cursed, then jerked her body against him, both his arms enclosing her powerfully. "Shut up," he said thickly. "Stop doing this to me. Oh, lord, Elizabeth."

She had opened her mouth to voice an instant protest, but the searing heat of his kiss trapped the sound somewhere in the back of her throat. Her fingers, curled into angry fists against his broad chest, straightened themselves slowly as her arms crept up around his neck.

A wave of dizziness swept over her and she could feel the flush heating her skin. In a split second, anger had become something else, and she was powerless to fight it.

The kiss was wild, hot, frantic. She could feel his arms pulling her closer, holding her tighter, and one of her hands locked in his thick hair while the other stroked the side of his face compulsively. A pulse in his temple throbbed violently beneath her fingertips, and she felt the shudder of his big body echoing her own tremors. His tongue stroked hers and his mouth was hard, demanding, taking something from her that she fought desperately not to give up.

But he was taking it, stealing it with a force beyond anything she'd ever known, and she could hear the silent scream of protest from somewhere deep inside her. Then that inner voice was silenced by the power of him, and she melted against him bonelessly with an anguished moan.

Her breasts were swelling against his chest, aching; her lips throbbed from the hungry, demanding pressure of his. She wanted to be closer to him, naked against him, wanted to feel his hands

and lips on her body. She wanted him with an
intensity that shook her to her soul.

She wasn't even aware of her tears.

But Kelsey was. He didn't know, even then, if
he could stop. His need for her tortured him,
knotting the muscles of his belly, aching in him
with a pain he had never known before. But her
tears hurt him more, the salt of them burning
him, and he drew back at last with a rasping
breath.

"Don't," he ordered, harsh, pained. His hands
were shaking, but he gently brushed the tears
from her cheeks. "Don't do that. I can't take it."

She was staring at him in the dimness, lips
parted, eyes gleaming darkly. "What?" she whispered, still unaware of the wetness of her tears.

"Cry. Don't cry. God, Elizabeth."

She drew a shaky breath. "Something broke,"
she said huskily, her voice puzzled. "I don't now
what it was."

He groaned and drew her back into his arms,
just holding her this time. She could feel his heart
thundering, his chest moving as though he had
run some terrible race. One of her hands rested
on his flat stomach, and she could feel the knot-
ted tension there; his entire body was taut,
rock-hard.

The heavy material of his black sweatshirt frustrated her; she wanted to feel his flesh, and her
fingers probed compulsively to search out the hard
ridges of muscle.

Kelsey caught her hand tightly in one of his.
"Don't do that," he said roughly.

She rubbed her cheek against his shoulder,
hardly aware of the gesture, "I want to."

"You don't know what you're saying." His voice was as hard as his body. The pain of his desire made him sweat and shake, and holding her was almost more than he could stand. But there was that tremor of warning inside him again, the sensation that something at the very core of him was swaying unsteadily on its foundations.

"I do know what I'm doing." And she did. He had been right; she *did* belong to him. On some deep level, in some part of herself she hadn't even known existed, he had already taken her. The force of him, the irresistible power he had channeled into that starkly intimate kiss had blasted through the barriers her rational mind had tried to erect. She knew now; that was why she had cried.

She lifted her head and looked up at him, wishing there was more light so she could see him clearly. "I know what I'm saying. And I know what broke."

"Elizabeth—"

"Me. I broke. So I guess I do want that scrapbook full of memories after all."

He was very still for a timeless moment, then cursed under his breath and got out of the car jerkily. He stood leaning against the side of the vehicle, silent and stiff.

She got out of the car more slowly, standing by the open door and gazing at him. "Just do me a favor, huh?" Her voice was soft, casual. "Don't send me any roses with the Dear Jane letter, okay? I hate to see roses cut." He wasn't looking at her, and she couldn't read his expression.

"You don't think much of me, do you?" he asked flatly.

Elizabeth stepped toward him. "You're wrong, you know," she told him. "So wrong. It's just that I know you won't be able to stay for long."

"Because I don't fit." His voice was remote.

"Is it so simple? No. But it would take more than any woman to hold you, Kelsey."

He drew a deep breath, but it didn't ease the tight pain in his chest, or stop the shaking inside him. "Forget it," he said in a hard tone that didn't quite hide the strain. "I don't want a sacrificial victim, Elizabeth. You think I could stand being with you *knowing* you were just waiting for me to walk out because you were looking at endings? No. No, I won't do it."

"If that's the way I made it sound, then I'm sorry." Her voice was still quiet, reflective. "You said yourself you'd be in my bed before the weekend was over."

"Because you belong to me." He couldn't stop the words.

"I know."

Kelsey turned toward her jerkily. "Then why the hell are you talking like this?" he demanded.

She reached up to touch his face lightly, feeling his jaw tighten. "I belong to you. But you don't belong to me." Her hand fell to her side. "I left my car across the road. I'll go home now. And let you do your job."

He stood for a long time where she'd left him, staring blindly at nothing. When he finally pushed away from the car and started back through the woods to meet Derek, he felt stiff and sore, and his chest was still hurting. When he reached the spot where his partner waited, he knelt down beside him and asked in a very tranquil voice, "See anything?"

"Nothing unexpected." Derek sent him a sidelong look, then turned his eyes ahead again. "The lady go home?"

"Yes."

After a moment, Derek suggested, "Maybe we'd better hit the road too. There's no way we can go into this place blind and hope to accomplish anything. Agreed?"

"Agreed." Kelsey sounded disinterested.

Derek didn't say another word until they reached the motel, and then he said only, "My room, if you don't mind."

Kelsey went with him to his room without protest or question, and sat in the chair by the window once they were inside. "Something on your mind?"

"You might say so." Derek sat on his bed, weighing his options and not entirely happy with any of them. Still, he didn't have much choice. Either he found a way to release some of the pressure building up inside Kelsey, or else he waited for the man to blow apart on his own—and who or what might get caught in that explosion?

"Well?" Kelsey was expressionless, but he was pale and still and coiled tightly.

Derek kept his voice level and impersonal. "I heard a story not so long ago that might interest you. It's about a kid who got involved in a dangerous business. A kid who went undercover for the first time, and had to watch without expression while his father's body was thrown off a freighter. I've wondered about that kid. I've wondered how he managed to get through it."

Kelsey's eyes lightened slowly, going very bright and hard, while his face remained still.

Derek noted the dangerous reaction, but continued in the same soft tone. "I think I understand. I think the kid just took twenty-one years of his life and locked them away in a split second. I think he locked those years away so completely that he doesn't remember he was ever anything but an agent."

"If you're trying to make a point," Kelsey said flatly, "I'm missing it."

"Yeah, you hate subtlety, don't you?" Derek almost smiled. "All right, then, I'll be blunt. I don't know what the problem is between you and Elizabeth, but I want to ask you something, Kelsey."

"So ask," he muttered.

"What do you let her see when she looks at you?"

Impatiently, Kelsey said, "What do you think?"

"I think she sees the only thing you've let anyone see in fifteen years. A chameleon. And you shed your skin to suit the circumstances, changing from one moment to the next. Becoming whatever you have to become. I think a woman needs a focus, Kelsey, and you're not giving her one."

"What are you . . . that you can do this to me?"

"Who are you? What are you? I know your name, but I don't know who you are. And I have to know who you are, because . . ."

"You can't catch the wind," she whispered. *"Chain the lightning. And you're as elusive as they are. Somehow, I know that."*

Kelsey understood, then, what Derek meant. And he understood why Elizabeth was so convinced their future together could be measured in days or weeks—but no more. She was simply responding to what she saw in him, understanding intuitively what he was only now seeing himself.

She saw what fifteen years of role-playing had made him. Derek's word: A chameleon. A man as changeable as the weather and, like the weather, an elusive force of nature which couldn't be controlled by anything but itself.

"Maybe I can't give her a focus," he said at last, with difficulty. "Maybe there isn't one to give."

"There will be, once you settle with the past," Derek told him, aware that Kelsey was no longer so tightly wound, that the pressure had eased. "Once you accept that you did what you had to do, that you were given no other choice."

"I don't know what you—"

"Yes, you do. The kid couldn't even grieve for his father, couldn't let out his rage and pain. And by the time he could, he'd already locked it away inside him." When Kelsey remained silent, Derek said, "It's over, finished. There's Elizabeth now, that lady who really got to you. And if you won't give her anything—how can you expect her to give you anything?"

A long moment passed, and then Kelsey said roughly, "Just where in hell did you study psychology?"

In a light tone, Derek said, "I'm a natural observer of human nature, the only thing I have in common with our esteemed boss. I'm also very tired. What's on the agenda for tomorrow?"

Kelsey let it pass, grateful for Derek's sensitivity. "More of the same, unless Raven calls. I'm a little curious about the possibility of military involvement; I may drive into Charleston and see what I can turn up."

Derek nodded. "I think I'll do a bit more reconnaissance out at Meditron. Maybe I can find a way into the place."

"Sounds good." Kelsey rose to leave, pausing at the door. "Thanks."

"Don't mention it."

"Hello, Ami."

She turned with a start and laughed. "You do like to sneak up on people!" But she was smiling, her haunting eyes bright. "Where have you been, Kelsey?"

He petted Lobo absently, accepting the dog's rumbling growl as a greeting. "Busy, little fawn. You, too, from the look of it. Riding so early?" He nodded toward the saddle hanging over the gate.

"I'm training for a horse show. That's where I was yesterday. You came to see Beth yesterday, didn't you?"

"Yes." He glanced past the girl at the quiet house. "Is she up yet?" It wasn't much past dawn.

"Sure. Beth gets up with the chickens. If you'll come into the house—"

He smiled at her. "How about doing me a favor and telling her I'm out here?"

"All right." She hesitated, a little troubled because he seemed different today. "Kelsey, is anything wrong?"

"No. No, nothing's wrong, Ami. Think you can hold down the fort if I kidnap Elizabeth for the day?"

She grinned. "Can I ever! Come on, Lobo, breakfast." She raced off toward the house, with the big dog obediently at her heels.

When Elizabeth came out of the house a few moments later, she moved slowly and a bit stiffly toward the man leaning against the pasture gate. She didn't know what to expect from him. In the small hours of the night she had quite literally thrown herself at him, and even though she had walked away from that confrontation, the rejection had been his.

What now? Which man waited for her so quietly by the gate? He was formally dressed in a dark suit, the image of a businessman busily climbing the corporate ladder, and she wasn't sure what to expect. Not sure at all.

She took a deep breath and walked steadily to him, painfully aware that just the sight of his big, powerful body was causing a riot in her own. There was still, somewhere inside her, a deep sense of shock that she could feel this way, but she had no weapon to fight the emotions and sensations.

Kelsey didn't say a word when she reached him. He simply drew her into his arms and bent his head to kiss her deeply and thoroughly. Elizabeth melted against him instantly, sliding her arms around his waist beneath the jacket, answering the demand of his lips with a fire of her own.

When he lifted his head at last, Kelsey was breathing a bit roughly. But he was also smiling.

She fought to catch her breath. "You—you changed your mind?" she ventured unsteadily.

"No," he murmured, reaching up to brush a

strand of her silver hair away from her face. "I'll still be in your bed by midnight."

Elizabeth blinked. "You're a very confusing man," she said at last, a bit helplessly.

"And I'm sorry about that." He was gazing at her face very intently. "Can you bear with me while I work it out?"

"I guess I'll have to." She was strongly aware of his body against hers. "You charmed my vicious watchdog, apparently mesmerized at least one of my sisters, and I won't even mention what you've done to me."

"Mention it," he requested, smiling.

"I think I commented once on the size of your ego; I'm not about to add to it."

He laughed softly. "All right, I'll let you off. This time. I need to drive into Charleston, and I'd like you to come with me. Will you?"

"Of course," she said simply.

Kelsey hugged her briefly, then stepped back. "I don't know what it is about you," he said conversationally, "but you've got the damndest habit of making me feel humble."

"Of making you feel *what*?" she asked, incredulous.

He met her laughing eyes, and his own were very bright. "Obviously, I don't do humble too well."

"That's one way of putting it."

"I'm not going to stand here and be abused. Do you need anything from the house? I'm ready to leave now."

"My purse. You can come in—"

"No. The next time I cross that threshold, I plan to be carrying you."

She tamed the leap of her heart and inquired gently, "Over one shoulder?"

"If necessary," he responded in a bland tone.

Elizabeth stood looking at him for a moment, smiling despite herself. "I'm out of my mind," she said finally.

"That makes two of us," he said lightly. "Go get your purse."

Kelsey remained where he was, watching her return to the house. Out of his mind, sure; why else would he torture himself by spending a nice platonic day in her company? She was so beautiful, it hurt him just to look at her, and the knowledge that her physical response to him was total had his control on the fine edge of impossible.

Out of his mind.

He had spent the remainder of a very bad night sleepless, trying with all his will to get a handle on the situation. His professional instincts told him to pull out, and quickly, because his own state of mind was too uncertain and that was dangerous; yet, pulling out now for whatever reasons would mean the death of his relationship with Elizabeth, because she would never understand why he had to leave. Not now. She couldn't see him clearly enough to understand his motives.

He couldn't leave her, not now, and that understanding had brought a cold weight to his stomach somewhere around dawn. Because unless this explosive thing between them was resolved, and quickly, he was a danger to all of them. With his mind and emotions in turmoil over her—to say nothing of his body—he would have to examine every instinct, every thought, to make certain they weren't colored by his feelings for her. And in a situation like this one, that hesitation could easily get somebody killed.

His partner's words in the small hours of the night made only too much sense, and Kelsey knew that Derek was right. How could Elizabeth trust a man she couldn't even see clearly? And until she learned to see him, and trust him, what was between them could never be completely resolved.

Kelsey knew what he had to do, but he didn't know how to do it. He honestly didn't know how to fuse the various bits and pieces of himself into a complete whole. How? How, when he wasn't sure what that complete image would be?

"So, you're still hanging around, huh?"

He looked at Meg, standing before him, and pulled his mind away from puzzles. She seemed younger this morning, more vulnerable; she was dressed in jeans and a sloppy sweatshirt, no makeup, and her hair was tousled. A very young sixteen-year-old.

"Hello, Meg." He smiled a little. "Yes, I'm still hanging around. Did you expect me to leave?"

She shoved her hands into the pockets of her jeans and looked mutinous. "I don't see why you're still here, that's all." Her tone was rude, deliberately.

"I hate to say wait until you're older, and you'll understand," he said dryly, "but I'm afraid I have to."

Meg smiled sarcastically. "Oh, right. Desperately in love with Beth, I suppose. Hate to tell you this, but you're just the latest in a long line of men dogging my sister's steps."

"I imagine that's true," he said neutrally. "She's a lovely woman."

Meg's eyes were bright and hard. "So they say. All of them. Blaine's still saying it, and he's been hanging around her for years. He'll be here when you're gone. She'll probably marry him, you know."

Kelsey wasn't putting much faith in his intuition these days, but he had a flash then and knew it was on target. Quietly, he said, "I won't take her away from you, honey."

Meg flushed to the roots of her pale hair. "You're damned right you won't!" she said shakily, and whirled to walk quickly toward the house. Her back was stiff, and she moved jerkily. She met Elizabeth on the front porch, and her high, unsteady voice was audible to the man watching several yards away.

"I don't see why you're wasting time with *this* one, Beth—he's just out for what he can get!" Then she vanished into the house.

Elizabeth hesitated, then came out to meet Kelsey, her face troubled. "I'm sorry," she told him.

"Don't be." He smiled a little. "The poor kid's just terrified of losing you."

She looked at him searchingly. "That's what I finally realized. I've dated in the past few years, and Meg's always hostile. Except to Blaine. I guess because he's so settled here, she's decided I wouldn't go far if I ended up with him."

Kelsey took her hand and began leading her to where he'd left his car at the end of the driveway. "Logical enough," he agreed calmly. "And I'd guess she's was also testing your authority to the limit. Any major trouble?"

Elizabeth looked down at their clasped hands

and had to swallow before she could respond. "No, not really. She runs with the wrong crowd, but so far I've been able to handle her. It's just a phase she's going through. She's a good kid."

Kelsey opened the car door on the passenger side, shaking his head. "You haven't had it easy."

She got into the car, smiling up at him. "I wouldn't have had it any other way," she said lightly.

He closed her door and went around to get into the driver's seat. "No, I guess not. You're not one to lean on somebody else, are you, Elizabeth?"

She half turned to look at him, studying his hard but somehow pleasant face. "I never have been. But then there wasn't anyone else," she added simply.

Starting the car and backing from the driveway, he said, "There is now. Keep that in mind, will you?"

They rode for a few moments in silence, and then she said, "Kelsey? Is Jo all right?"

He reached over and took her hand, closing his mind to the inevitable speculation of a mind that knew too well what dangerous men could do to a captive. "I'll make sure she's all right," he said steadily, making a reckless promise he had every intention of keeping.

He would make very sure that Jo Conner was just fine. And if that was a promise broken for him, nothing in the world would be able to repair the shambles he'd leave of Meditron and everyone involved.

"With your trusty sword?" she said softly.

"With everything I've got."

•   •   •

"That's it."

Josh looked over one of Zach's shoulders, while Raven looked over the other, and it was she who spoke after reading the computer's screen intently.

"No wonder they had the data locked. Is that as dangerous as I think it is?"

Josh answered. "Deadly, in the wrong hands. And if they're holding that girl captive, I'd say it was in the wrong hands."

"So what do we do with this?" Raven asked.

"We get it to Kelsey, pronto," Zach said, turning away from the computer as the other two straightened. "Luc's checking with his sources now, but if that data on Major Thorn checks out, there's one hell of a bad situation brewing down there."

Josh looked at him thoughtfully. "You're the only one of us with military experience. Just how much authority can Thorn command?"

Zach grunted. "All he wants, dammit. The military set up a nice little operation in Pinnacle, and it's been running smoothly for years. Thorn's kept it quiet and produced for them, so they've stopped keeping an eye on him from the higher levels. Soldiers are a peculiar breed, Josh; they've been trained to take orders and not ask questions. Except for maybe one or two key people, Thorn's men probably don't even know he's going into business for himself. And it's a lead pipe cinch they don't know a girl's being held hostage in the plant."

Softly, thinking as much of the phone call she had received as of this new information, Raven said, "Kelsey and Derek are going to need help." She was gazing steadily at her husband.

He met her gaze, his own still thoughtful, but didn't respond immediately because Lucas walked into the room. "Is the information confirmed?" he asked his investigator.

"In spades." Luc rested a hip on the corner of a desk and addressed the others briskly. "Thorn's a renegade, all right. He has a history of doing things his own way, and promotion was denied several times due to quote, unauthorized activities, end quote. I'd like to know who the hell was dumb enough to put him in charge at Meditron. I played a hunch and got in touch with a friend who works both sides of the streets."

"Weapons dealer?" Zach asked neutrally.

Lucas, knowing that the big security chief hated arms dealers, gave him a rueful look. "Don't bite me, but yes. To his credit, he's one of the few who has scruples; he won't sell to just anybody. He told me that he'd heard a renegade army major was looking for buyers for some very sophisticated weapons—and that *he* didn't care who he sold them to as long as the price was right." Luc shook his head. "And it will be. There are groups out there who'd pay just about anything."

"Who takes care of shipping?" Josh asked.

Zach shrugged. "Thorn, I'd bet. He's got the authority to ship stuff out of there. Who's to know the destination isn't what it should be? This country sends arms overseas all the time."

"Wouldn't Meditron's quota come up short?" Raven asked.

Zach gestured disgustedly toward the computer. "You read that. Thorn's been shaving the quota for months; he reports machine breakdowns and design problems. He could have a huge stockpile by now, and he probably does since it looks like he's getting ready to sell the stuff and get out."

"Then we don't have much time," Raven said.

"Less than you think," Lucas said quietly. "My friend told me something else. Our renegade major has sweetened the pot. Along with the more conventional weapons, he's offering a nuclear missile—with the warhead intact."

There was a moment of silence, and then Raven said softly, "Dammit, I'll bet that's why Mallory's keeping quiet if he isn't in on this. Thorn must have threatened to use the missile."

"That makes the timing more critical." Josh looked at his wife and friends for a moment. "Zach was right. We can't all go down there."

"Teddy stays here," the big man said definitely.

"Want to bet?"

They all turned to look toward the doorway of the computer room, where Zach's small redheaded wife leaned casually.

"You stay here," Zach told her in a voice that would have vanquished most armies.

Teddy smiled at him gently, an understanding smile that did nothing to dim the laughing triumph in her brown eyes. "I got the floor plan," she said serenely.

Josh lit a cigarette, focusing all his attention on the matter. Raven studied her fingernails intently. Lucas gazed thoughtfully at his shoes while whistling softly under his breath.

"Where the hell did you get it?" Zach demanded.

Her eyes danced. "Think I haven't been paying attention to how you commandos work? I spoke to a friend of a friend, and then I called in a few favors."

"Then you'll give it to me," Zach told his wife firmly.

"If I did that," Teddy said reasonably, "you'd refuse to let me come along. Besides, it's in my head, and I think I'm going to have a hard time remembering it until I actually *see* Meditron with my own eyes."

"This is serious, Teddy," he said very softly.

Equally softly, she said, "I know it is. Another jungle. And you're not going into it without me."

Judging that the time was right, Josh said briskly, "Luc, you know General Ramsey, right?"

"Yeah. Kyle knows him, too. Want us to run interference?"

"We'll need it; try to keep him from throwing a battalion at Meditron before we have a chance to get in there quietly. And we may need a favor or two from the good general."

"You've got it," Luc said.

"Hagen needs to know," Raven noted reluctantly.

Josh nodded. "We'll let Rafferty and Sarah beard that lion, and keep him busy long enough to give us some time."

Zach was still gazing steadily across the room at his wife. "The rest of us head south?"

"The rest of us head south, first thing in the morning," Josh confirmed. He glanced at Zach, then took Raven's hand and gestured to Luc; the three of them left the room.

Teddy crossed the room until she stood before her husband. "You knew I would," she said gently.

"Dammit, Teddy!"

She didn't resist when he pulled her down into his lap. And since there were always better things to do than fight . . .

Teddy loved storms.

"Why are we stopping?" Elizabeth glanced around at the location where Kelsey had chosen to park the car, puzzled to discover that they were in one of the worst areas of Charleston.

He was intently studying a small group of men several yards away on a street corner and answered absently, "Those guys are ex-military. They may know something."

"Military? How can you tell? And—are you saying the military is involved at Meditron?"

He looked at her, his eyes still abstracted, then smiled. "I can tell because they have the look: bits and pieces of uniforms and a certain way of moving. And, yes, we think the military might be involved. My partner talked to a lady who saw a couple of soldiers at Meditron."

She absorbed that, then asked, "Even so, how could those men know anything? Pinnacle is miles away—"

"If the military *is* at Meditron, they're being quiet about it. Given that, I'd expect the personnel to spend their off-hours in the nearest city of any size. And that's Charleston. They wouldn't be noticed here by civilians, but other military or ex-military personnel would probably spot them. We'll see."

Elizabeth looked at him, rather unnervingly formal in his dark suit, and asked uncertainly, "Will they talk to you?"

Kelsey's eyes flickered, then he smiled again. "Why don't I go find out?"

But he didn't get out of the car for a moment.

First, he shrugged out of his suit jacket and tossed it into the back seat. His tie quickly went the same way. He unbuttoned his cuffs and rolled the sleeves up to show bronze forearms, loosened the tail of the shirt at his waist to give a baggy appearance, and then unfastened several buttons at his throat.

It took Elizabeth a moment to realize what he was doing, and it fascinated her. The only comment she made, however, was when she saw a flash of silver at his throat. "Dog tags? Were you in the army?"

"No." His tone was absent, and he quickly ran fingers through his thick hair to make it curiously disarranged. "Wait here, all right?"

"All right." Elizabeth watched him leave the car, her eyes widening unconsciously. And in that instant, she understood why Kelsey had been an agent so long and why it was so difficult for her to bring him into view.

Within three strides he had subtly altered his entire way of moving. There was a guarded slouch to his shoulders, and he walked with the careful, graceful stride of a man who had made it a habit not to be heard. There was something taut about his body, something leashed—and something that was very definitely lethal. Despite his snowy shirt and neat pants, by the time he reached the men he looked like one of them.

He *was* one of them.

Elizabeth rolled down her window and strained to hear, somehow unsurprised to find that Kelsey had fallen into the rough, coarse jargon of the streets. His tone was arrogant, his voice hard and harsh. His guarded posture eased a bit as the men responded to him almost instantly, and there was suddenly an atmosphere of camaraderie among all the men.

Utterly fascinated, Elizabeth watched and listened for nearly an hour. She realized that the men had recognized a kindred spirit in Kelsey, a man who had walked the same jungles and felt the same pain as they had—if not with them, then before or after them. Like a skilled actor, he had submerged himself in a role, and the result was so totally right that these men trusted implicitly that he was one of them.

She began to understand him then.

Six

When Kelsey returned to the car, there was a gleam of satisfaction in his eyes. He started the car and drove away, absently rolling his sleeves back down. "Well, now. I think we're getting somewhere."

"What did they tell you?" She was gazing at him intently, realizing that he had thrown off the role the instant it was no longer needed. He was relaxed again, his posture straighter but somehow looser, his face tranquil.

In a brisk tone, Kelsey said, "For years now, there have been soldiers billeted on the army base here, but they don't work on the base. They work outside Charleston, in three shifts. All of them are single men, all career army, and a good half of them officers with scientific or technical backgrounds. None of the officers at the base are talking about it at all, but the grunts think weapons are being manufactured in a big way somewhere nearby."

"Grunts?" She thought she knew, but wanted to hear his explanation.

Kelsey grimaced faintly. "Sorry; it's hard to lose the jargon. A grunt is your garden-variety soldier or non-commissioned officer. A sergeant or below in rank. Got it?"

"Got it." Elizabeth forced herself to concentrate on something other then Kelsey, something equally important—at least until Jo was safe. But she was so fascinated by him. "Then they may be manufacturing arms at Meditron?"

"It's a good bet."

"Legally?"

Kelsey shrugged. "I imagine the military made a deal with Mallory. Everything aboveboard, legal if not exactly ethical since the town of Pinnacle apparently isn't aware of it. It's possible they're making something more chancy than conventional weapons, but, if so, I'd expect them to be making conventional weapons as well—probably rifles and handguns. Maybe one or two bigger guns; Meditron just isn't large enough for much more. If they're doing anything experimental, it has to be on a limited scale; security out there wasn't entirely military until a few weeks ago, and if they were screwing around with some of the exotic stuff, it would have been military all the way. If it was authorized, that is. It's obvious the military set up their little show years ago, so I believe it was intended for conventional weapons production. And everything went fine for a few years. But, recently, something went wrong."

"What was it?"

Frowning a little, Kelsey said, "If I had to guess—
and I do—I'd say somebody decided to go into
business for himself. Guns are a very hot-selling
item these days, and a man with the authority to
ship them could make himself a fortune rather
quickly. Those guys back there told me they
thought a major was in charge of the off-base con-
tingent; they've seen him, and they read him as
being dangerous."

"Would they know that?"

"Sure. When you're in the army long enough,
you learn to recognize a good commander. Soldiers almost always know. And the military has
its rotten apples, just like any other large organiza-
tion."

Elizabeth was silent for a moment, then said,
"Does that mean some army major is holding Jo?
But, what reason would he have? Why would he
do such a thing?"

"I don't know why he picked her, but I have to
believe he needed some insurance. If Blaine Mallory
realized recently that something was wrong and
had decided to report the matter to whomever
was responsible for setting up the operation, the
major may have decided a hostage would stop
that, or at least give him some breathing room.
What bothers me now . . ."

"Is what?"

Kelsey sighed roughly. "Hell, Mallory has the
county cops in his pocket, and they outnumber
the security at Meditron. Even if he didn't want to
risk alerting the military brass, he could have his
boys surround Meditron and force the major to
give up his hostage or face the kind of attention
he can't want. There must be something else,

some other threat keeping Mallory quiet. If there's some exotic stuff being produced out there, and if the major threatened to use it somehow—"

"You don't think Blaine would be quiet just for Jo?"

"At first, maybe. Until he had time to think. He has a reputation for being highly intelligent; once he calmed down, he'd think it through. And it's reasonable to decide that in this particular situation Jo's best chance lay in as many people as possible knowing she's being held. So why didn't he sit tight and just blow the whistle? Granted, the military hates to wash its dirty laundry in public, but there are half a dozen bases in this general area, and they'd move fast to stop one of their own who'd gone bad."

"Maybe he didn't have any proof? How could he? Just his word and Jo missing."

"That wouldn't matter. In a situation like this, the military brass would be suspicious as hell, and they'd want answers fast. At the very least, they'd send . . ."

Elizabeth waited for a moment, then said, "Send what?"

Slowly, Kelsey smiled, and his eyes were suddenly very bright. "They'd send somebody to Meditron to check it out. I need to talk to Mallory."

They remained in Charleston for a while, however, since Elizabeth called Blaine Mallory and discovered he was "out of town" for the weekend. The information bothered Kelsey, but it was something beyond his control so he didn't waste much time worrying about it.

He had taken his work as far as he was able for

the time being, and even though his inner clock was ticking in a louder and faster rhythm now, warningly, he was grateful that there was time to be with Elizabeth and think about them almost exclusively. She seemed very thoughtful and quiet, gazing at him often with reflective eyes, and he had the unnerving feeling that he had done something he wasn't entirely aware of doing. Something that was making her look at him in a new way. But she said nothing until they had finished lunch and were lingering over coffee in the restaurant.

"Where did you get the dog tags, Kelsey?"

He looked at her across the table, glad that his smooth tip to the headwaiter had produced this secluded table. He always found it difficult to take his eyes off her, but when they were alone it was even harder. And she was so lovely, dressed in a simple white blouse and dark blue skirt, her hair up. So lovely it broke his heart.

"Kelsey?"

He cleared his throat. "Sorry. The dog tags? Oh, I've had them for years. Props, you might say. They come in handy sometimes."

Elizabeth nodded slowly. "And you just happened to bring them along on this job?"

Kelsey felt a little uneasy, and wasn't sure if it was his professional or his personal instincts warning him. Alarm bells were going off *somewhere*. "Well, yes. In an unknown situation, you never know what you might need."

Very softly, she said, "Different every time you look. Like mercury. Like a cat. Or a chameleon."

After a moment, he said, "Ah. My role playing back there."

"It was amazing," she told him. "You took off your jacket and tie, rolled up your sleeves—and you were an ex-soldier. Just like that." She snapped her fingers. "You looked like one of them, spoke like them, moved like them. Within a matter of seconds, they *believed* you were one of them."

"An agent's stock-in-trade," he said lightly, growing more uneasy. What had she seen? And why had that bit of role playing by him sparked this reflection and curiosity? If he was right in believing that his changeable nature had confused her, why would one more change apparently settle something for her? And what had been settled? He felt a tightness constrict his chest, and recognized the feeling as fear.

Elizabeth was shaking her head slowly. "Completely instinctive. No one taught you how to do that; it isn't something you can teach. You didn't think about it, didn't plan. You simply became someone else."

After a moment, with difficulty, he asked, "And that bothers you?"

She tilted her head a little to one side. "I . . . I don't know. I think I understand you a little better now. But you're like quicksilver, Kelsey. I see you, and yet you're never the same as you were the last time. I think I'm afraid that . . ."

"What?" He wasn't sure he wanted to know.

"That it's more than roles. That you've learned to be elusive to keep others from getting too close. And if that's what it is—"

He reached across the table and took her hand. "If that's what it is," he told her steadily, "then I'm trying to change it because of you. I'm not doing it deliberately, Elizabeth, please believe that.

I'm not trying to shut you out. That's the last thing I'd do willingly. I want to be close to you more than I've ever wanted anything in my life."

"But, can you?" she asked quietly. "I don't know, Kelsey. You've spent almost half your life in a very dangerous business, and I'd guess you learned to adopt that protective coloration out of extreme need." She paused, then finished softly, "I know you don't want to hear this, but it doesn't make a difference to me. If you can't let me get close, if you decide you just can't be a part of my tame life, I'll understand."

Tightly, he said, "I told you—I don't want a victim."

Elizabeth smiled. "I'm not a victim. Haven't you realized it yet, Kelsey? I'm in love with you."

He could feel his heart stop and then begin hammering somewhere in his throat, and swallowed hard before he could speak, aware again of something moving slowly, shuddering, inside him. "What about everything you've been saying since we met? That there hasn't been enough time?" His voice was rough.

"That was stupid of me, wasn't it?" She was reflective. "I've never been in love before, you see. And I never expected it to happen so fast. But it has happened, Kelsey." She gazed at him, her eyes incredibly gentle.

There was a tightness in his throat. He couldn't swallow now, and couldn't even begin to control the violent emotions tearing at him. Wild in passion, she was wondrously sweet and vulnerable in love, and he was desperately afraid that the violence in him would harm that. He was lost somewhere in her vivid eyes, realizing only then, in that moment, how lonely his autonomy had left him.

"I called home before I tried to get Blaine," she told him. "The girls are spending the rest of today and tonight with friends. They'll be in school tomorrow. The house is empty. Why don't we go back there."

He drew a deep breath, and his voice was strained when he forced words out. "Elizabeth . . . I want you so badly I can barely think straight, but I have to know that *you* know who'll be in your bed."

"I do know." She smiled that incredibly tender and loving smile, her vivid eyes darkening. "A chameleon."

"Dammit, I don't—"

"Kelsey." Just that, just his name, softly.

He swore, bitterly and under his breath. Then he made an economical gesture and a waiter appeared as if out of thin air with the check.

It was only sheer luck they didn't get a speeding ticket.

Kelsey was driving with both eyes fixed steadfastly on the road before them, both hands on the wheel; he knew if he so much as glanced at Elizabeth, they'd never make it to the house. And when he spoke, his matter-of-fact words were belied by the hoarseness of his voice.

"Do you know what you're doing?"

She was sitting a little sideways, watching his face as fixedly as he watched the road. "I know."

"I don't want to leave you with a scrapbook full of memories." Still matter-of-fact.

"I'll cross that bridge later."

"You've already crossed it, in your mind. How long are you giving us, Elizabeth? A week? A month?"

"We'll have what we have."

"And then?"

"Now who's looking at endings?" she murmured.

"Answer me, dammit."

She sighed almost inaudibly. "What do you want me to say, Kelsey?"

"The truth." His hands gripped the wheel, white-knuckled. "You've thought about it, I know. You expect me to leave; what then? Will you marry the shark you know? Settle down in your tame little town and raise a few kids a well as sisters and peaches? And keep a scrapbook somewhere in your mind with memories of your one wild fling? Is that what you've decided?"

"Don't."

"Why not?" His voice had quickened, become sharp and hard. "A man likes to know where he stands. Is that my role this time, Elizabeth? Is that why you've held Mallory off all this time, so you *could* have that wild fling with someone just breezing through your life? No ties, no promises, just a little scandalous sex before the settled life you want?"

The car fishtailed a bit when he slammed on the brakes and stopped abruptly near the house on the dirt driveway, dust flying, and even as he turned off the engine Elizabeth was out of the car and running to the house.

Kelsey sat there for a moment, hating himself, knowing he was a bastard for what he'd said to her. He tried to tell himself it was for the best, that he had been forced to say those things so that she would realize what she was doing, but the mental assurances were hollow. He was a bastard. He had hurt her, and he was hurting too much himself not to know it. Slowly, he got out of the car, removed his tie, shrugged out of his jacket and tossed them into the back seat, then headed for the house.

He wouldn't be carrying her over this threshold after all, he told himself somberly as he opened the screen door and went inside. Not in passion, or playfulness, or commitment. Not today. Maybe not ever.

"Elizabeth?"

She didn't answer, and he went from room to room, searching. She wasn't in the house. The back door was open, and Kelsey stood gazing out for a moment, before making his way to the barn. It looked like a tumbledown structure, but when he passed through the open door he saw that it was sturdy, and smelled the sweet scent of new hay in the loft above him. "Elizabeth?"

"Up here."

A narrow stairway led up into the loft, and he went up slowly. Bales of hay were stacked neatly along the three walls of the loft, leaving a space in the center about the size of a small room. Loose hay cushioned the floorboards there, and Elizabeth was sitting very still in the middle of a bright quilt spread out over the hay. She didn't look at him, and her voice was soft when she spoke.

"What's the euphemism? A roll in the hay? But hay isn't very comfortable, so I got this quilt from the house. I knew you'd come after me, Kelsey.

You had to. You're as much a prisoner of this as I am."

He made this way to where she sat, forced to keep his head bent to avoid hitting it on the beams above him. He knelt down before her, hurt even more by the controlled expressionlessness of her delicate face. "Honey—"

"I won't marry Blaine. I don't know what I'll do . . . after. No matter what you believe, this isn't something I planned. But I want you, Kelsey. Is that so wrong? Is it something I should be afraid of, or ashamed of?"

"No."

She looked at him, her eyes luminous, deep. "I realized something today. I realized that I haven't done anything just for myself in ten years. I haven't made a single decision without stopping to consider how it would affect my sisters or the business. I don't regret that. I made that choice. But now isn't it my turn, Kelsey? Can't I decide—about this—just for me now?"

Gently, he said, "You know better than that. This decision affects me too."

"You want me."

Kelsey half closed his eyes. "Lord, yes, I want you. But you believe I'll leave you."

Her eyes were bottomless.

"Kelsey, whether you'll leave me isn't something either of us can predict. You can't even say it. You can't say you love me. Can't say you won't leave me one day. Even though you want to say it—and I can see it in your eyes—you can't. You aren't sure yourself."

She was right, and he knew it. He had known since those lonely predawn hours when he had faced too much of himself to ever be able to go back again. "If I said it, and then I had to leave—"

"I know." Her voice was infinitely gentle. "It would haunt you, just the way your father's death has haunted you. You had to turn away from that final look at him, even though you loved him. You had to walk away from him. And if you found you had to leave me, had to walk away from someone else you loved, it would haunt you."

Kelsey drew a shuddering breath, trying to ignore pain and confusion. Did it matter that he hadn't said it? It shouldn't matter; what existed was real, voiced aloud or held silent. Yet, somehow, it mattered. "I think—" He cleared his throat roughly. "I think I'll miss my deadline."

"In my bed by midnight?" She reached out to lay a hand on his thigh just above his knee. "I don't think you'll miss it."

He looked down at her hand, knowing that his muscles had tautened instantly, that his belly was knotting in a sudden rush of hot desire. His skin felt flushed, and breathing was suddenly very difficult. "Elizabeth, I don't want to be remembered as the man who tore your life apart."

"You'll be remembered as the first man I ever loved."

Kelsey caught his breath, and whatever it was that had held him back until now splintered in the force of what he felt. "We're both being too damned fatalistic," he said thickly, reaching out to grasp her shoulders, rising on his knees as he pulled her up against him. "I control my own destiny, dammit, and if I want to stay with you, I'll *stay* with you!"

Her arms slid up around his neck and her body

swayed to meet his in a movement as natural as a sunrise. "Just be with me now," she whispered, her lips feathering along his jaw. "Just be with me as long as you can."

"Oh, hell, Elizabeth." But neither her fatalism nor his own apprehension about the future could stop the building chain reaction of desire and willingness. Kelsey's mind told him that a physical consummation with so much left uncertain between them was dangerous, but the warning was a faint voice lost in the roar of something far more basic and sure than intellect.

And when her mouth opened beneath his, when her full breasts pressed to his chest, when her hips moved in a subtle, unconsciously seeking movement against him, the faint voice of reason was utterly silenced.

The kiss, like the one the night before in the car, was hot, frantic, compulsive. His lips slanted across hers and his tongue thrust starkly in a possession that could never satisfy either of them. They both wanted more, bodies straining to be closer, arms wrapped tightly around each other. For an eternal moment they remained locked in that embrace, the kiss too wild to be reined. Then Kelsey drew away with a rough sound and rose to his feet, pulling her up with him.

It was instinct that kept his head bent to avoid the overhead beams, instinct and the driving need to go on exploring her soft skin. He was pulling her blouse free of the skirt even as her hands shakily tugged his shirt loose, and the softness of her throat drew his lips like a lodestar.

"Kelsey . . ." The skirt slid down over her hips and legs to pool around her feet, and her fingers coped with the buttons of his shirt blindly. And there was something driven in the breathless rush of her voice. "I want you . . . so much . . . I can't stand it anymore. I can't wait."

He groaned when she impatiently sent the last two buttons flying, sweeping his shirt open so that she could touch his chest, his hard stomach. She helped him remove her own blouse and the cream-colored bra, rising on tiptoe instantly to press her breasts against his chest. Kelsey held her against him hard for a moment, his breath escaping raggedly as twin points of fire seared his chest. And he lost what was left of his breath when he felt her hands slip between them to fumble at his belt.

"Easy," he murmured, capturing her wrists and pinning them gently to her sides, knowing he was too close to the edge to take much more.

"No," she said huskily, her lips moving against his shoulder. "I won't let you change your mind again."

His laugh was a rasping sound. "Honey, I couldn't change my mind if it was the price of my next breath."

"Good." Her lips feathered along his jaw and fleetingly brushed his mouth, then she stepped back and bent to skim the flesh-colored panties down her legs and then gather her discarded clothing and toss the bundle to one side of the quilt.

He kicked his shoes off, hardly noticing that one landed down in the barn hall, his own fingers fumbling at his belt as he watched her unselfconscious grace. "God, you're beautiful," he said thickly, watching her breasts lift as she reached up to free her hair, so that it fell around her tanned shoulders in a curtain of spun silver. Her breasts were honey gold tipped in rosy brown, the nipples hard with wanting him. Her waist was tiny, hips flaring gently in perfect curves, and her legs had been made by Nature to give a man wistful dreams.

Kelsey had always been of the opinion that most bodies required a judicious draping of material here or there, since few perfect examples of the human form could be found. Elizabeth was the only woman in his experience who was actually more beautiful totally naked than clothed. Silver and gold, her vivid green eyes pools of enchantment, standing before him the way a woman should stand before a man, all grace and pride and with knowledge born in the caves glowing in her eyes.

He was hardly aware that he had shed the remainder of his clothing, and it was only when he felt the quilt beneath his feet that he realized he had stepped closer. One hand lifted, and he traced a lingering line across the slopes of her full breasts. "No bathing suit pallor," he murmured hoarsely.

Elizabeth didn't move, but her eyes were heavy-lidded, her lips parted. "Outside my bedroom window," she whispered, "there's a little balcony. I sunbathe out there when I'm alone."

"In the nude."

She half nodded, the wild ferocity of that unhooded falcon growing more intense in her eyes. "In the nude. Does that shock you, Kelsey?"

He could feel something fluttering in the back of his mind, some response, a sudden understanding. Softly, he said, "I don't know why I had you figured as small town conventional. You aren't that at all, are you, Elizabeth? You made yourself fit because you had to, but your spirit is . . . wild."

She lifted her arms slowly until her hands slid around his neck. "Wild enough to catch a chameleon?" she questioned in her breathless, driven voice.

"We'll find out." It was almost a groan, and he pulled her against him, blindly finding her lips.

He didn't know if he had drawn her down to the quilt or she had guided them; it didn't matter. The thick quilt and layer of hay beneath cushioned them, and he lost himself in her. She was so utterly responsive, so wildly hungry for him, and the simmering fire between them exploded in a raw detonation just as he had believed it would.

Whatever violence existed in him was more than matched by her passionate response, and Kelsey stopped wondering which of them would be burned by the fire. They were both burned.

If he had stopped to think about it, Kelsey would have been astonished that he could rein his own desire even temporarily, but she was as curious and entranced by his body as he was by hers, and somehow their bodies allowed them the time to explore.

He surrounded her breasts with his hands, his thumbs probing the hard nipples before his mouth found them, her soft sighs and murmurs a siren song in his ears. And he could feel her hands exploring, her nails occasionally raking softly so that his muscles writhed like living things beneath her touch. He realized on some distant level of his mind that her fingers paused at every scar, tracing slowly, but not even the evidence of his dangerous past was enough to cool the fire.

Elizabeth held him, breathless and dizzy, ripples of heat spreading through her until her skin burned and her body was aching and restless. She probed his shoulders and back compulsively, feeling coiled muscles that were a stark indication of physical strength and power, feeling here and there a rough area, a puckering of his bronze skin indicating a scar. There was a long scar just beneath his breastbone, another low on his stomach and ridged by muscle. Some distant part of her wanted to acknowledge her understanding of the battle scars he wore; she wanted to cry at the pain of his past, the marring of a beautiful male body, but she could only whimper aloud at the emotions and sensations tearing through her own body.

"Kelsey . . ."

He was breathing harshly, his face intent, fixed in expression. One hand left her breasts to stroke over her quivering belly, lower, and he caught his breath even as she did. "Lovely. So soft and warm," he said in a thickened voice. "Elizabeth, my Elizabeth."

"Yes." The restless ache was building, becoming more than she could stand, and she writhed suddenly with a gasp. "Yes! Yours, Kelsey . . . make me yours."

A harsh sound escaped him, and Kelsey buried his face between her breasts for a moment. "I can't wait," he muttered as he lifted his head. "I need you so much, I can't wait."

Elizabeth caught at his shoulders as he rose above her, slipped between her thighs. She felt a seeking touch, warm and hard, and a fleeting moment of purely instinctive panic vanished as her body responded wildly to the touch of him. His mouth covered hers in a fiery kiss, and even as his tongue possessed her mouth, his body moved in a slow, powerful thrust to possess hers.

She barely felt the slight, quick pain; all her senses were caught up with the throbbing fullness of him inside her. The sensation was wild, strange, heated. She had lost her breath somewhere along the way, and her body held him with a tightness she could feel as well as he could.

Kelsey caught his breath with a rasping sound, his eyes closing briefly, and even through the hot veils of passion he realized something. But nothing could have stopped him in that moment, and when her body sheathed him totally with its tight heat, he forgot everything but spiraling hunger.

She moaned deeply, arching up to meet him as he began moving, the feverish heat inside her burning until she couldn't stand it. She lost control even as he did, matching his hot rhythm with her own wild response, hearing his groan and her own whimpering cries and feeling the primitive need to fuse their bodies together until nothing could ever tear them apart. He could never be hers except by his own will, but her body claimed his for all time and she knew there would never be another for her.

The hot, sweet tension coiled unbearably and yet she wanted it to last forever. But her body surged toward release, desperate, driven, and when it came at last in a blinding, shattering explosion she cried out wildly, barely hearing Kelsey's ragged groan of pleasure.

• • •

His weight was wonderful, and Elizabeth murmured a protest when he would have left her. He
eased up on his elbows, still breathing roughly,
gazing down at her flushed, contented face.

"Did I hurt you?" he asked huskily.

In a dreamy voice, she said, "I didn't notice."

Brushing a strand of her silver hair back, he
said, "Dammit, why didn't you tell me?"

Elizabeth didn't pretend to misunderstand. Smiling a little, her eyes darkened, she said simply,
"You would have changed your mind again."

Even though his mind and instincts had balked
at the thought of Blaine Mallory having been Elizabeth's lover, Kelsey had never even considered
the possibility that no one had been. And when
he told her that—somewhat severely—she laughed
and raised her head to kiss his chin.

"Thanks a lot."

Kelsey shook his head helplessly "You're just so
damned beautiful! If I'd been around, you wouldn't
have gotten out of *high school* without me as
your lover."

"But you weren't around," she murmured, smiling. "And I was never much impressed by the
sexual revolution. If it didn't feel right, then it
obviously wasn't right for me."

He shook his head again, bemused. "If I'd been
thinking at all a few minutes ago, I would have
thought you'd had a least one long-term relationship behind you. You were so—so natural."

"Because I belonged to you," she said matter-of-
factly. "I felt completely natural."

He was obviously troubled by that, and she lifted
her head to kiss him lightly.

"Stop brooding," she ordered in a gentle tone. "I love you too much to ever regret this. Ever. No matter what happens."

"Elizabeth . . ." He lowered his head to kiss her, the first tenderness almost instantly becoming something else, and they both felt the stirring of need again.

Raising his head, Kelsey half closed his eyes and caught his breath when he felt her inner muscles immediately tighten around him. A bit thickly, he said, "For an inexperienced lady, you sure know what you're doing."

Elizabeth smiled a slow, unconsciously sultry smile. "Just doing what comes naturally."

Kelsey approved wholeheartedly.

Seven

"Where the hell's my shoe?"

Folding the quilt neatly, Elizabeth gave him an innocent look. "I think it flew down into the hall. You didn't seem to be paying attention at the time."

"I was being seduced," he retorted, going to the edge of the loft to look downward.

Hearing his half-conscious curse, she said, "Horses *do* leave evidence of their presence, I'm afraid."

Kelsey looked at her. "Uh-huh. And, of course, my shoe would have to land in the middle of some of that evidence."

"Life's like that."

His humorous, slightly pained expression became suddenly intent as he looked at her, and Kelsey came back to her and framed her face almost completely in one large hand. "I don't know what I did to deserve you," he said quietly, "but it must have been something terrific."

Elizabeth swallowed hard and smiled up at him, her heart aching. "I'm glad you think so. Just don't brood about us anymore, all right?"

"I can't help it." His fingers were moving, stroking her face almost compulsively. "I want to stay with you. I want to sleep with you and watch you in the morning. I want to see you smile and hear you laugh. I want to *be* with you."

It was not something she could help him with, and Elizabeth knew it. Only Kelsey could decide if she fit into his future. She could love him and wait for him to work his way through what he was feeling. And she was very aware that he could decide, in the end, to leave her . . . because he had to. Because that elusive part—or parts—of him would be unable to be content in her settled life.

Thinking of that now, as she had several times before, she said slowly, "There's something I want you to know, Kelsey. I wasn't lying when I said that if you left me, I'd understand. I'd understand because you were right when you said earlier that I made myself fit here. I was very young and I didn't really have a choice, but it was a painful struggle. I *know* what you're feeling . . . if only in a small way. I know how hard it is to rein something wild. Even now, after ten years, I have to let it out sometimes.

"But you . . . You've been in a dangerous business for fifteen years, nearly half your life, and what you've learned to be in that life isn't something you can just walk away from and dismiss. It's a part of you, a very strong part. A part I love. Don't change. Don't change for me or anyone else."

With difficulty, he said, "And if what I am drives me away from you?" Something he had reluctantly already faced, though it hurt terribly. The possibility that he might one day have to leave her.

"Then you can't let that tear you apart," she said steadily. "You said—you didn't want to be remembered as the man who tore my life apart. You won't be, no matter what. I love you too much for that to happen. But there's something *I* won't be remembered as, Kelsey. I won't be remembered as the woman who tore *you* apart."

After a moment of gazing into her determined eyes, he lowered his head and kissed her gently. "I'll try to keep that in mind," he said huskily. "Just don't let me hurt you." It was a rough, strained plea.

She touched his cheek fleetingly and then turned toward the stairs. What could she say to that? Nothing. "It's getting late; it'll be dark soon. Let's get your shoe out of the muck and go up to the house."

Her words were light, and ten years of controlling a tendency to wildness kept her expression serene. Elizabeth knew she would hang onto that control as long as necessary. She would not, for one instant, show him the ache she felt. He would never leave her willingly; she felt that and was warmed by it. He would fight his own nature to stay with her, if she let him. But she wasn't willing to let that happen.

If he came to terms with himself and discovered that he loved her too much to leave her, and if he emerged from that struggle whole and healed, she would be happier than ever before in her life.

But if he found, in the end, that what he needed she couldn't give him, she would wave goodbye and provide a place here he could come back to if he wanted. Here in her tame life. And she'd never let him see the scrapbook full of memories she was already lovingly putting together in her mind.

She wouldn't be remembered as the woman who tore Kelsey apart.

He carried her over the threshold. He also carried her up the stairs to her bedroom, and except for a couple of forays down to the kitchen to stave off starvation, they spent the entire night in bed together.

Kelsey awoke in the hours before dawn, vaguely aware that this particular time seemed to be his own personal witching hour; it seemed that just before dawn he was always facing things he would rather have avoided. But he woke to find himself holding Elizabeth tightly and possessively, and even though she slept deeply and was obviously undisturbed by the strength of his embrace, he forced his arms to relax a little.

And, because he had to, because he knew despite her control that Elizabeth did indeed need a promise from him, he faced himself once more. He allowed himself to remember the memories of fifteen years, beginning with his father's death. And, like still photographs flipping rapidly through his mind, a complete picture of those years emerged.

He remembered the bad things, of course. Friends lost, assignments that had snowballed beyond his or anyone's control and had gone haywire. Harried interludes of time spent in dangerous places doing dangerous things. Countless brushes with death. Roles assumed easily at need and just as easily discarded. The face of every criminal he had helped to capture, and some who were killed.

He remembered crowded, dangerous cities and vast, lonely oceans and breathtakingly beautiful tropical islands. He remembered glittering parties and silent stakeouts and cold jails. He remembered partners who had saved his ass. He remembered too many eleventh-hour rescues, too little sleep, too many guns. Food that tasted of cardboard eaten hastily in cars or dark motel rooms or on the run. Hours spent hunched over a computer keyboard looking for any single tiny item of information required to topple some criminal kingpin.

And . . . no real regrets.

He regretted lives lost, and there had been times that, looking back now, he regretted he had not acted more quickly or more effectively. But for what he had done with his life, he had no real regrets.

And now?

Kelsey held this warm, vital woman in his arms, thinking of her falcon's eyes and practiced control, of the tenderness and love in her that could explode into a passion so total it could—and did—steal his breath and stop his heart.

"I won't be remembered as the woman who tore you apart."

Something inside him shuddered, swaying on an uncertain foundation.

It was a long time before he slept again.

• • •

"Do you think it will work?" Raven asked quietly, her voice so low that only her husband heard.

Sitting beside her in the efficiently soundproofed and decidedly luxurious cabin of one of the company Lear jets, Josh took her hand and didn't answer for a moment. His tumultuous courtship of Raven having altered his life in many ways, he no longer felt the need to pilot himself whenever he flew somewhere; though still habitually cautious as most wealthy men had learned to be, his obsession with keeping control of the smallest details of his life was virtually a thing of the past.

"You'd have a better idea of that than I would, darling," he reminded her at last.

Raven sighed, her worry about Kelsey increasing even as the miles between them and Pinnacle lessened. "I told you what Derek said when he called me. Kelsey's right on the edge this time; he may not be up to playing another role."

"I could go in with Zach," Josh noted after a moment in a very neutral voice.

Her eyes were grave, her smile understanding, but Raven shook her head. "On the edge or not, Kelsey would *never* allow that to happen. If something went wrong, you'd be worth more to the major than anything or anyone else he could get his hands on. You know that, Josh."

Josh knew, but he grimaced faintly. "I guess. Well, maybe Kelsey's partner can go in."

"Derek's good," Raven acknowledged. "But he doesn't have Kelsey's chameleon nature. Derek is Derek—no matter where he is or what he's doing, he's always the same. Kelsey is whoever he wants to be."

"Which is why he's on the edge this time?"

"That's what Derek thinks, and I agree. I knew it would happen some day. For the first time in fifteen years, someone important to him has looked Kelsey in the eye and asked who he is—and after so long, he isn't sure."

"It makes sense." After a moment of silence, Josh said, "What *is* his other name?"

"I don't know."

He looked at her. "Really? And you worked with him for five years?"

"Uh-huh." She smiled a little. "Hey, it's a secretive business, remember? You learn early not to ask too many questions."

Josh sighed and glanced toward the rear of the plane, where Zach and Teddy were deep in conversation. Then he looked back at his lovely wife and smiled, his normally rather hard blue eyes softened. Soon they were glowing, as always when they focused or her. "Well, whoever he is, we'll help Kelsey. We all owe him a hell of a lot. I know he doesn't care about that, but I'm glad it's our turn to back him up."

"If we can," Raven reminded.

"Oh, we can. It only remains to be seen how *much* we can, and how well we can."

Hagen, who considered himself a veritable maestro with all matters secretive, clasped his pudgy hands together over his straining paunch and stared broodingly at his spotless desk. This situation, he decided silently, had all the earmarks of a truly nasty mess.

The military's mess, of course, and he had expressed all the proper pious sympathy when he had called General Ramsey to commiserate. Being Hagen, a smile creased his cherubic face when he thought about that satisfying call; he and the military were more often than not at loggerheads, and it was enjoyable to see them squirm.

Still. It was a serious matter, a potentially deadly one, and quite a number of lives were at risk. That sobered him.

It probably wouldn't have surprised Josh much that Hagen knew much more about the matter than anyone—including Rafferty and Sarah—had seen fit to tell him.

He had his sources, after all.

That Hagen had decided privately not to send anyone else into Pinnacle despite the nuclear threat was primarily due to his knowledge and understanding of all the persons already present or en route to Pinnacle.

Regretfully, he acknowledged the fact that he was unlikely to be able to utilize the talents of Long and his men on any future problems; though Sarah Lewis still worked for his agency, the only real tie remaining between that talented and inventive group of extraordinary people and his agency—was Kelsey.

And the very fact that Kelsey had not reported in, nor gone through official channels for the information he had required told Hagen more than his agent would have liked. Told Hagen, in fact, a great deal.

Really, Hagen though vaguely, he should turn his talents toward matchmaking on a grand scale. He seemed to be good at it.

Dammit.

• • •

Elizabeth was rather fascinated by Kelsey's elusive partner, introduced to her simply as Derek. A big man like Kelsey, he was blond and startlingly handsome with lazy eyes and a faintly drawling voice. He had arrived late in the morning after being called by Kelsey, and they were all three sitting in the living room with coffee, planning.

And Derek fascinated Elizabeth because she had the unnerved feeling that nothing she or anybody else could ever say or do would surprise him. There was something in those lazy eyes that was older than time, infinitely tolerant, and faintly amused.

"Sounds right to me," he said now as Kelsey finished explaining the conclusions he had come to, lighting a cigarette.

"Mallory's on his way over here," Kelsey told him. "Elizabeth called him."

Derek cocked an eyebrow. "Going to deck him?"

Elizabeth giggled despite herself.

Kelsey frowned at both of them, but his eyes were bright. "No, I'm not going to deck him. Unless he provokes me," he added as an afterthought.

"The way you feel about him," Derek murmured, studying the glowing end of his cigarette, "a polite good morning would provoke you."

Kelsey ignored that. Pointedly. "I want to know why in hell we haven't heard from Raven. That isn't like her."

"I imagine we could call the jet."

"Jet? What jet?"

"Company jet. A Lear, I think. Hard to know which one they'd take, though. There are—what? —six or so in Long's fleet?"

After a moment of silence, Kelsey sighed. "Do you know for sure they're coming down here, or just guessing?"

"Calling it an educated guess. I know Raven, and from what I've heard of her husband and that crew of his, they wouldn't just offer information or advice. They'd come down here suited up and ready to get in the game."

"They wouldn't *all* come," Kelsey protested.

"All who?" Elizabeth asked, bewildered.

There was amusement in his eyes, but Kelsey sighed in a long-suffering manner. "Once upon a time, I had a partner named Raven. She was good, damned good. But one night she accidentally knocked a man flat on his back in a hotel hallway, which rattled him so much that he proposed to her."

"Marriage?" Elizabeth asked, smiling.

"Orange blossoms and all. Unfortunately, Raven was in deep cover working an assignment, and I was on the sidelines providing backup. The man, to the consternation of us all, turned out to be Joshua Long. Heard of him?"

"Who hasn't." Elizabeth's eyes widened. "I suppose he didn't just dismiss her from his life?"

"Hardly. When she gave him the slip—being undercover and in a rather dangerous position—he promptly called out his bloodhounds. A lawyer, an ex-marine security chief, and an ex-cop turned investigator." He reflected broodingly. "Things got kind of crazy after that. Anyway, at some point our esteemed boss Hagen caught them in a weak moment and deviously swore all four of them in as federal agents, and has spent the past year and more drafting them one by one to help him out."

"Is that legal?" she wondered.

"It isn't ethical," Derek murmured, blowing a smoke ring and studying it critically.

"They don't care," Kelsey told Elizabeth. "It's a bit odd in this day and age, but all four of those men are dragon slayers. Zach's the only one of them who really *looks* the part, but all four swing a mean sword."

"You left out the best part of the story," Derek complained mildly.

Kelsey gave his partner a suspicious look. "And what part did I leave out?"

"Matrimony." Derek looked at Elizabeth and said lazily, "Each of those men emerged from his respective assignment with a wife in tow. I understand Hagen is beginning to consider himself quite a matchmaker."

"I thought you didn't know the story!" Kelsey said accusingly.

"A little bird must have told me."

"And I can guess her name, I suppose."

Elizabeth decided not to comment on that aspect of the story. "They sound very unusual. What about the women?"

Kelsey returned his attention to her, feeling his body and senses react just to looking at her and no longer surprised by it. He cleared his throat determinedly.

"Well, Raven was in this business for a number of years, so she certainly knows the ropes; and she's a dragon slayer by nature as well as training. Rafferty—he's the lawyer—married another of Hagen's agents; Sarah does research primarily and doesn't seem to care too much for field work. Zach—the security chief—married a redheaded spitfire who stumbled into an assignment he was on; Teddy looks more like the princess being rescued from the dragon, but she swings a pretty sharp sword herself. And Luc—the investigator—married a lady named Kyle, who is very beautiful, very bright, and very courageous; she wouldn't wait to be rescued either."

Elizabeth, fascinated, felt a distant throb of pain when she realized that each of those extraordinary men had apparently found women who matched them on every level and who were perfectly capable of going into battle with their men.

And she suddenly felt inadequate. Kelsey had seen and done so much; he was an epic dragon slayer in his own right and had been for fifteen years. What was she? She, who raised sisters and peaches, lived in a small town in the back of beyond, and when danger had threatened, had sat back biting her nails and waiting for someone else to act.

Swing a sword? She couldn't even find one to lift!

"Excuse me," she said suddenly, and escaped to the kitchen on the pretext of getting more coffee.

She stood in her safe, bright little kitchen, staring around at the familiar haven that was her tame little world.

The wildness inside her had always been controlled before now, escaping momentarily in brief winging periods, and settling quickly afterwards. Like the owner of some rare and fragile bird, she had opened the cage, let it out, and strictly controlled the limited flight, calling it quickly back before it could totally escape. But the passionate time spent with Kelsey had, she realized vaguely, changed something.

She couldn't get the cage door shut this time, not completely. And the bird, with a new kind of freedom sampled, wanted more. Much more.

And a tiny, wise voice from deep in her mind—or her heart—whispered that her only means of truly understanding the man she loved lay, not in him, but in herself. Kelsey flew by instinct, never returning to a cage but only to some more settled part of himself, and if she were to ever fully perceive the man he was, she would have to learn to fly that way as well.

She wasn't even sure that what had been caged and tethered for so long could take wing completely now in total freedom. She wasn't entirely certain that she had not, after all, forgotten how to really fly.

But her love was stronger than her fear.

Elizabeth had barely disappeared into the kitchen when Kelsey and Derek heard a car in the drive.

Derek lifted a questioning brow, and Kelsey shrugged. "I don't suppose it matters now," he told his partner, replying to the question of Derek's anonymity. "Mallory will have to know who I am, so he might as well meet you. We need his cooperation too much to waste time with games."

"Okay by me," Derek murmured.

Kelsey went to the front door, which was standing open, and held the screen door back as Blaine Mallory stepped up onto the porch. Keeping his voice cool and unthreatening, Kelsey said, "Good morning. Would you come in?"

Mallory's face darkened. "You've certainly made yourself at home, haven't you?"

Kelsey felt the hairs on the nape of his neck stirring, but held on to tranquillity. "I would have been disappointed if you hadn't noticed. This way." He led the way into the living room, introducing Derek, who rose politely, as his partner.

Blaine Mallory stood staring at both men, his face expressionless, eyes cold. "Where's Beth?"

"In the kitchen making coffee," Kelsey told him. He leaned lazily against a chair, and continued speaking in a calm, but subtly more authoritative tone of voice. "My partner and I work for a federal agency, Mr. Mallory. We received a tip and came to Pinnacle to investigate Meditron."

Mallory lifted a disbelieving brow.

They stood confronting one another, neither noticing that Derek had returned to his chair and lighted a cigarette while he thoughtfully studied them.

After a moment of strained silence, Derek said mildly, "Marquis of Queensberry rules, or just a glorious free-for-all?"

Kelsey blinked, glanced aside at his partner, and realized abruptly that his own posture had become decidedly stiff and alert in response to Mallory's hostility and his own. He forced himself to relax, looking back to Mallory. "I don't think it needs to come to that," he said, addressing his partner's remark. "Mr. Mallory has the reputation of being an intelligent man. And we all want the same thing."

"Which is?" Mallory asked flatly.

"Jo Conner free. The renegade major out at Meditron locked up in a stockade, with his toys defused." The last was a guess, but Kelsey knew he had struck a nerve when Mallory's eyes widened slightly.

After a moment, Mallory said, "How do I know you're who you say you are?"

Kelsey crossed his arms over his chest and sighed. "A reasonable question. The answer is— you don't. Oh, we could show you identification. But everyone knows you can have those things made up in most novelty shops for a couple of dollars. I could give you the number of our home office, but since we aren't listed anywhere you only have my word for it that you *would* be calling a federal agency."

Mallory's mouth twisted slightly. "You don't inspire a lot of trust, know that?"

Softly, Derek said, "You could call the military brass in Washington. It's what you wanted to do in the first place. And they'd come tearing down here whether they believed you or not. They probably wouldn't be too subtle about it, but it *would* bring the situation out into the open."

"And blow Pinnacle off the map!" Mallory snapped.

Neither Kelsey nor Derek betrayed, by so much as a flicker, that Mallory had just confirmed their guesses.

Reasonably, Kelsey said, "He can't possibly believe the threat would stall you much longer. The point is that if he's crazy enough to make such a threat, he's crazy enough to blow Pinnacle off the map anyway just to cover his tracks."

"It'd be a hell of a diversion," Derek noted.

"Diversion?" Mallory weighed his options rapidly, and came to the conclusion he needed help. Like it or not, he had to trust these men. "Diversion?" he repeated. "I don't think you've realized it yet, but Thorn's missile is nuclear—and the warhead is intact with a specialist standing by just waiting to launch the thing."

In the act of lighting another cigarette, Derek went still, his hooded gaze lifting swiftly to Mallory's strained face. "Damn," he said softly.

Kelsey's expression had gone grim. "Thorn must really be out of his mind," he said tautly.

Mallory ran fingers through his hair, looking suddenly older and exhausted. "He is. The missile is experimental—a prototype. It was designed, only God knows why, to be used on an extremely close target. The man who designed it called it a suicide device; it's meant to be some kind of final resort. Maybe to destroy a command post or an intelligence center before it could be overrun by the enemy." In a wry comparison, he added, "I suppose it's something like the Rebels burning Atlanta before the Yankees could get it."

Kelsey shook his head. "That's the damndest— How's it launched?"

"It's sitting on its launch pad right now. Maximum range is twenty miles; minimum . . . hell, you can turn on the timer and just walk away. If it's launched and impacts before the timer runs out, the impact triggers it. If there's no impact, but the timer is activated, it detonates when it reaches zero. And if it were to be launched now without activating the timer, it would still detonate on impact."

"And it's aimed at Pinnacle?" Derek asked.

Mallory nodded.

"The military didn't okay it?" Kelsey asked.

"Hell, no. Thorn okayed it. The specialist—a physicist, I believe—is a buddy of Thorn's. He built the thing in secret at Meditron, and Thorn plans to sell it to the highest bidder, along with a huge load of conventional weapons. My contract with the military specified *only* conventional weapons manufacturing on a limited scale; they brought in the necessary personnel and I supplied the buildings. Meditron still manufactures medical equipment in two buildings, but the other four are for military use."

"How did Jo Conner get involved?" Kelsey asked.

"My fault." Mallory sighed. "I was mad as hell when I found out about the missile—and about Thorn shaving his quota and stockpiling weapons. I told Jo more than I meant to, and she went looking one night. I'd already threatened Thorn that I meant to call Washington; he grabbed Jo before I got the chance."

Mallory was a little pale now, and his eyes were dark and hard. "That bastard's got her in the same building as the missile, with the *specialist* tinkering with the damn thing constantly."

"You're sure the warhead's intact?" Derek asked.

"Positive. Or, at least, that it's radioactive. That's enough for me."

"Me too," Derek agreed dryly.

Kelsey thought carefully, gathering the questions they needed answers to. "Does Thorn stay at Meditron at night?"

"Always. He hasn't left the place in more than two weeks."

"The guards at the front gate are his?"

"Yes. They allow nobody in without a pass except me, and when I go in they always alert Thorn. Each of the four military buildings has individual security with soldiers posted inside monitoring the cameras outside each building. The doors to those buildings can only be opened from inside; there are no windows."

"Ventilation?" Derek asked.

"The system is completely enclosed; there's no way of getting in through an airshaft." Mallory had realized what they were trying to find out and briskly supplied the information. "The buildings were built years ago; they have concrete walls reinforced with steel. There's a skylight in Building Three—where Thorn's got the missile—but the roof's covered with pressure plates that set off alarms if they're touched."

Kelsey looked at his partner. "So. We go through the front gate, or we don't go in."

"Are *you* crazy?" Mallory demanded. "When I go in he holds a gun to Jo's head and waits for me to breathe too hard. And his specialist buddy is standing by the missile with a finger poised to launch the damn thing. If you came anywhere near—"

"If two federal agents came anywhere near him," Kelsey agreed, "he'd likely go completely off his rocker. But he's a military man no matter what else. Career army?"

"So he said."

"The army," Derek noted idly, "is very big on inspections. Unscheduled inspections."

Mallory's eyes narrowed. "You think he'll fall for that?"

"Why not?" Kelsey shrugged. "If you are sitting blamelessly at your desk, or else loudly threatening Thorn that you're going to call the brass, he'll think you haven't acted as yet. And if Derek and I show up for one of those spot inspections . . ."

"He wouldn't show you the missile," Mallory objected.

Kelsey frowned. They needed advice from some- one who understood the military mind. "Derek, are you ex-service?"

"Not military service," Derek responded cryptic- ally.

"Mallory?"

"No."

Kelsey cursed softly. "Neither am I. We need someone who is. We have to have a good idea of just how Thorn'll react to an inspection. Whether he'd push the panic button, or just shift the mis- sile around or hide it. He has to have a contin- gency plan for inspections; he wouldn't be caught off guard by something that likely."

"The last inspection at Mcditron," Mallory noted thoughtfully, "was about six months ago."

"So he'd be ready for another possible inspec- tion, wouldn't he?" Kelsey shook his head. "If we only knew—"

"Then ask an expert," a new voice suggested cheerfully.

Kelsey turned quickly, finding Raven smiling at him. Behind her in the doorway of the living room were Josh, Zach, and Teddy

"We knocked," Josh offered. "You were appar- ently too absorbed to hear."

Completing introductions, Kelsey was wryly amused to note that Blaine Mallory, though clearly not overly impressed by federal agents, was cer- tainly very impressed by Josh Long. He also gave Zach a distinctly wary look, and regarded the two women with baffled interest.

"How'd you find the house?" Kelsey asked Raven.

"Derek."

Kelsey frowned a little, but understood when Raven stepped closer and touched his arm lightly.

"You okay, pal?"

After a moment, Kelsey smiled. "So he called you about me?"

"He was worried."

"Well, I can't really blame him for that."

Raven smiled, but her eyes were sober. "So answer my question. Are you all right?"

"Getting there."

Raven knew when not to push. "Glad to hear it, pal. Now, why don't you introduce us to his lady of yours. She is here, isn't she?"

Raven's questions fell into a silence in the room, and Kelsey felt a sudden crawling chill. He looked at Derek, thoughts tumbling through his mind like leaves in the wind.

Derek, his face unusually still, glanced at his watch and then looked back at Kelsey. "Too long," he murmured.

Eight

I'm sorry, Kelsey, but I have to help Jo.
I love you.
Elizabeth.

They found the note on the refrigerator, and Kelsey swore in a soft, bitter monotone while he read it. He felt cold and afraid, and his mind was numb. And, somewhere deep inside him, the solid walls shaken again and again since he had first met her shuddered a final time and collapsed.

He loved her. Dear God, how he loved her!

The others were quick and efficient in discovering that Elizabeth had taken her horse rather than her car, and it was Raven who remained close to Kelsey while precious moments were spent in making certain of her disappearance.

"If she took the horse," Blaine Mallory said finally when they were grouped in the living room again, "she's already there."

Raven was watching Kelsey's white face, and her voice was calm and matter-of-fact. "Then we assume she is. Kelsey, did she know what you were planning to do?"

"Yes." He was staring at the note in his hands. "She knew Derek and I would try to bluff our way in."

"Then she'll be ready for that," Raven said approvingly.

"And we came prepared." Josh's voice was also calm; he had considerable experience in dealing with men on the brink of deadly emotional explosions after more than fifteen years of knowing Zach. "General Ramsey was delighted to provide us with military uniforms and identification, two complete sets. One is for you, Kelsey, and the other for Zach, since he's ex-military and knows quite a bit about explosive devices." He looked at Derek with a lifted brow. "Do you object?"

"No. I don't know much about bombs."

Zach, having just returned from their car, handed Kelsey a garment bag and said, "The car's outfitted with military decals and otherwise looks the part. I say we don't waste any time."

Kelsey looked at him for a moment rather blindly, then said, "Yes," and went away with him to change into the uniforms.

Josh looked at Mallory. "You know where Jo Conner is being held, and where the missile is?"

"Yes."

"Teddy—"

"Right. Mr. Mallory, if you'll help me, I think we can draw a diagram for Zach and Kelsey." She asked the man to come over to the couch, and they both bent over the paper Teddy was rapidly sketching on.

Derek joined Raven and Josh, and looked at Kelsey's former partner questioningly. "What do you think?"

Raven was chewing on a knuckle. "I think we'd better get those ladies out of there fast."

"Can Kelsey handle it?" Josh asked her quietly.

"That's the question, isn't it?" She sighed worriedly. "I just don't know. If he hasn't been too shaken up by all this, he'll automatically fall into the part. But if he's started doubting himself, or if he's too worried about Elizabeth . . ."

"Her timing," Josh noted dispassionately, "is rotten."

Derek smiled a little. "Not necessarily. It'll be a dandy diversion. And, between us, we may be able to overload Thorn until he isn't thinking clearly. He certainly won't have a lot of time to move his missile *and* Jo out of sight."

Raven looked at him straightly. "Can *she* handle it? You've met her; we haven't."

"She can handle it," Derek replied calmly.

That obviously settled the question for Raven. "Good. She's probably demanding to see her sister. I would be. And Thorn will very likely take her to where Jo is."

"He hardly seems the type to balk at two hostages," Josh agreed. "Not with a missile pointed at a nice little town."

Raven nodded. "And I imagine Elizabeth will keep him occupied until Kelsey and Zach can arrive. So far so good."

"Unless," Derek said, "Thorn folds under the pressure and does something stupid."

Wincing, Raven said, "You could have gone all day without saying that, friend."

Josh glanced at his watch. "The evacuation ought to be underway by now."

Derek blinked, and his handsome face looked impressed. "Evacuation? Of Pinnacle? How the hell did you manage that?"

Smiling a little, Josh said, "Once General Ramsey was convinced that this whole thing couldn't be swept under the rug, he got busy. Military personnel from Charleston are moving everyone quietly out of the town."

"And if someone alerts Thorn?"

"They can't. Power and phone lines to the town have been cut, there are military roadblocks, and jammers make it certain that no one could radio Meditron if they wanted to. The military might emerge from this with a black eye, but nobody will be able to say they didn't move the citizens out of danger before sending in their—er, representatives—to tackle Thorn."

"Neat," Derek said in approval. He looked at Josh with amused, considering eyes. "Must be nice to have clout."

"It has its drawbacks," Josh retorted.

"For instance?"

Raven cleared her throat. "Well, General Ramsey wasn't at all willing to have to admit that civilians went in to clean up a military mess, so he, uh, reactivated Josh and Zach."

"Come again?"

"When Zach was discharged, he was a master sergeant," Raven explained. "He's now officially a major in the reserves. Josh, who was a major in the reserves, is now officially a colonel."

"Should I salute?" Derek asked Josh gravely.

Josh scowled at him. "Not on your life. And don't try it with Zach either; he considers it to be a personal affront that he was booted into officer country—even in the reserves—without so much as a by-your-leave. I think he's going to have words with General Ramsey when this is all over."

Derek looked at Raven. "They don't favor the structured military life?"

"They don't favor *any* structured life unless it's their structure."

"Ah." Derek nodded with perfect understanding.

Josh gave his wife a severe look. "I just don't like taking orders, that's all."

"Of course not, darling."

Jo Conner was tall with short pale hair, a face as lovely as her older sister's, and bright blue eyes. Bright blue eyes which were presently snapping with rage.

"Thorn, you're out of your tiny mind! If you think Blaine will sit still with Beth held here—"

"He sat still while you were held." Major Thorn was a man of medium height and a slight build somewhat disguised by his erect military carriage. He was about forty with brown hair going gray and gray eyes that were flat and hard.

After the first relieved embrace of her sister, Elizabeth had stood silent in the small room that had been Jo's jail for the past two weeks and just listened. She felt incredibly alert and energized and, curiously, not frightened. Kelsey would come, and she meant to make certain that her presence here would help rather than hinder his efforts to stop this madness.

"You threatened Blaine," she said now, gazing at the man who was holding a town unknowingly hostage; he had wasted no time in explaining his little toy to her. "But you can't keep him under your thumb forever. You'll push him too far."

Thorn looked at her, smiling. His cold eyes were considering. "You're Mallory's woman, aren't you?"

"No."

Jo gave her sister a swift look, brief confusion replaced suddenly with curiosity.

Thorn was nodding. "Oh, yes, you are. I've heard the talk. He'll sit still while you're being held. I'll put a gun to your head and watch him sweat." One hand dropped to caress the army Colt he wore in a webbed holster.

Elizabeth felt a chill. "You can't hope to get away with this," she said evenly.

Thorn found that highly amusing. "My dear, I *have* gotten away with it. All I need are a few more days to finalize arrangements, and I'll be sunning myself on some lovely tropical beach."

The guard outside Jo's room knocked briefly and stuck his head inside. "Call from the gate, sir. Could be trouble."

"Excuse me, ladies," the major said politely, and left the room briskly.

"Beth, what—"

"Shhh!" Elizabeth glanced around quickly. "Did Thorn bother with bugs in this room?"

Jo blinked. "I know every inch of this place," she said with some feeling. "Four walls, a locked door, no windows, an army cot, and a stack of very old magazines. There's a bathroom through there—" She pointed toward a closed door "—without even a mirror. Believe me, this place is *empty*."

It hardly seemed reasonable to Elizabeth that Thorn *would* have bugged the room: What could he hope to gain by doing so? But she kept her voice low on the off chance. "Listen carefully, Jo. Two federal agents are going to try and bluff their way into the compound; we have to be ready."

After a moment, Jo backed up and sat on her cot, staring blankly at her sister. "You're serious?"

A little dryly, Elizabeth said, "Thorn has a nuclear missile pointed at Pinnacle—what do you think?"

"Okay, okay." Jo shrugged, the expression on her face revealing her sense of helplessness. "This whole situation's felt unreal to me since they tossed me in here and started serving me lousy meals on a tin tray three times a day. What's Blaine doing?"

"Helping the agents. I hope."

"You don't know?"

"I left before he got to the house. They were waiting for him there."

Jo gave her a look. "Want to tell me why you're not Blaine's woman anymore?"

"I never was," Elizabeth said mildly. "It isn't my fault that people assumed."

Slowly, Jo started to smile. "The federal agent! In two weeks? You fell in love with a federal agent in two weeks?"

Elizabeth had a sudden impulse to burst out laughing. It all sounded so insane! "No, not in two weeks. Since Friday."

"This *past* Friday?"

"Uh-huh."

Jo's smile became a grin. "Must be *some* federal agent!"

Elizabeth smiled in response, unaware that her eyes had softened. "He is. He certainly is."

Jo studied her for a moment, then nodded. "Great. Can't wait to meet him. But, for now—what do we do? Do they know where we're being held?"

"Blaine knows, doesn't he?"

"Yes."

"Then he'll tell them."

Jo frowned, "Will he? Blaine isn't exactly a team player, you now."

"He'll tell them."

"Your federal agent won't take no for an answer, huh?"

"Something like that."

Jo accepted Elizabeth's opinions. "Okay. So how do we help them get us out of here and take the teeth out of that fanged monster in the next room?"

Elizabeth took a deep breath and exhaled slowly, thinking of the makeshift "plan" she had devised on the swift ride to Meditron. Risky. Lord, yes, it was risky. But the right amount of confusion at a judicious moment could just tip the scales in their favor—and in Kelsey's.

"We create a diversion," she said calmly.

Josh peered through the binoculars, watching the unobtrusive dark car approach the gates of Meditron. "Everybody cross your fingers," he said softly.

Beside him in the concealing shelter of the trees,

Raven, Derek, Teddy, and Blaine Mallory waited tensely.

Raven had one eye on her watch, but murmured, "Nobody's seen Kelsey's car, right?"

"Nobody here," Derek answered. "It'll work."

"They're soldiers," Mallory protested. "It's too simple a trick to fool them—"

"They're men," Derek corrected calmly. "Name me one man who wouldn't abandon more than a guard post to help two lovely ladies in distress, and I'll show you a statue."

"Zach's going to have a fit," Teddy noted, but not as if the prospect of her very large husband in one of his rare bursts of anger frightened her.

"That's why we didn't tell him about this part," Raven said dryly. "Ready?" she asked Zach's wife.

"Yes, just—Derek, hand me that gun, will you?"

He did, rather gingerly.

Raven grinned at him. "Still the phobia about guns?"

"They make a lot of noise," he said severely, apparently not noticing Blaine Mallory gazing at him in astonishment.

"I'm ready," Teddy announced, having secreted the wicked little automatic.

Josh reached a long arm to hug his wife hard, and kissed her very thoroughly. "Watch yourself, darling."

"Always." Raven touched his cheek, and then she and Teddy disappeared into the woods heading for the main road.

"I thought all federal agents carried guns," Mallory said, clearly baffled.

"You've been watching too much television," Derek told him.

• • •

Zach was driving, as comfortable in his major's uniform as he had been wearing sergeant's stripes. He glanced at Kelsey as he turned the car into the drive leading to Meditron. He didn't like the look of his friend whose white face and stricken eyes revealed too well the fear that gripped him.

Intentionally harsh, Zach said, "If you want to give the show away, just keep looking like somebody kicked you in the stomach, Kelsey."

Kelsey turned to him. "You're a bastard, you now that?"

"You won't get an argument."

After a moment, Kelsey stared straight ahead and, seeing the guardhouse, tensed. "Sorry, Zach," he murmured.

"Don't mention it, Colonel."

Slowly, Kelsey squared his shoulders. His face, though still pale, relaxed and became somehow faintly arrogant and impatient. His posture altered subtly. And within seconds, he seemed to *become* a colonel.

Watching from the corner of his eyes, Zach was impressed. "Raven said you were good," he muttered.

"Let's just hope I'm good enough," Kelsey said, and even his voice had changed, becoming cool and authoritative.

Zach rolled down his window as the car stopped at the gate, and watched the cautious approach of a very young "security guard." Two more men remained inside the bulletproof guardhouse, watching alertly. In a slightly bored tone, Zach said, "Open the gate, soldier, and tell your CO he has visitors."

"Identification, please," the soldier requested, torn between wariness and dismay as he looked at the car and Zach's formidable bulk.

Zach flashed his and Kelsey's ID cards, making certain the soldier couldn't get his hands on them. "Damn these inspections, sir," he said to Kelsey, but loud enough for the soldier to hear. And then, more directly to the soldier, "The Colonel hasn't got all day."

"I'll just call Major Thorn," the young soldier said nervously. "Standard procedure, sirs."

Kelsey leaned over to give the soldier a good look at him, and his voice was impatient. "Open the gate, soldier."

"Begging the Colonel's pardon, sir, but I'm under orders to admit no one without Major Thorn's—"

Very gently, Kelsey said, "Son, if you don't want to be walking guard duty at our embassy in Moscow, you'll open the damned gate."

The soldier saluted hastily, his face wiped clean of expression. "Right away, Colonel."

Zach, who had gazed meditatively through the windshield throughout the exchange, smiled a little as they drove through the open gate. "Sure you were never military?" he murmured.

Kelsey was glancing back over his shoulder. "They're calling Thorn," he said.

"We knew they would." Zach frowned a little as he pulled the car into a parking place fairly close to the building they were most interested in. "What bothers me is that those kids back there are awfully jumpy. If something goes wrong—well, they just might shoot first and think about it later."

"Chance we'll have to take." But Kelsey wasn't happy about it either. Elizabeth was in there.

With fifteen years of autonomy behind him Kelsey had never wasted much time in thinking personal thoughts during these infiltrations of enemy territory. He just concentrated on his job, untroubled by flashes of things left undone and regrets and memories that other agents dealt with.

The chameleon, once solidly in his camouflaged skin, was autonomous, invulnerable, alone.

But not this time.

He had known from the moment of reading Elizabeth's note that everything had changed. The walls inside him, protecting his inner self from even his own examination, had crumbled. And what he saw inside those fallen walls, though still not entirely focused because he'd hardly had time to consider, was himself.

Stripped of all ability to hide where she was concerned, he was achingly vulnerable, raw. He was . . .

He was the man who loved Elizabeth.

"Kelsey?"

Holding consciously to his chameleon's skin for this one last vitally important interlude, Kelsey opened his door and got out of the car. "Ready," he said to Zach, and hoped he was. Hoped with everything inside him.

"Could you help us, Lieutenant?"

"Corporal, ma'am." The very young soldier didn't even realize he had betrayed himself; he was *supposed* to be an ordinary security guard rather than a military man. But then, no part of his training had covered this situation. What was he supposed to do when fate deposited two stunningly beautiful women at his post and had them appeal to him with lovely, helpless gazes?

The redhead with the huge amber eyes was standing on one side of the car looking down at a very flat tire and chewing her bottom lip, and the tall, striking brunette stood on the other side smiling at him.

"Ma'am—"

"It just went flat," the brunette explained with a shrug. Her violet eyes were glowing. "And neither of us has ever changed a tire in our lives! Do you think one of you could—?"

The young corporal found himself elbowed aside as both the other guards left the guardhouse. "But—"

"Come on, Phil," one of them said sarcastically, "d'you really think these ladies are a threat? They need help, for Pete's sake!"

Unhappily, Phil followed them. What was a good soldier supposed to do?

"Got a jack?" one of the others asked the redhead.

She handed him the car keys with a smile. "I guess it'd have to be in the trunk, wouldn't it?"

Phil's two comrades opened the trunk and bent forward to get the jack and spare, conveniently shoved far back in the trunk, neither of them noticing that the brunette quietly approached them from behind.

Phil opened his mouth, but froze when he felt something poke him in the middle of his back.

"I wouldn't," the redhead said softly as her free hand nimbly plucked his automatic from the holster. Phil saw a potentially glorious career going up in smoke.

"I can't find—" one of the other men began, then banged his head on the trunk lid as he straightened hastily in response to his own gun being efficiently removed from its holster.

While he was holding his head and swearing, the second man tried to pivot and draw his gun. A hard kick to the back of his leg sent him to the ground in a cursing heap. And he looked up at the striking brunette with sad, disillusioned eyes as she held a hand out commandingly for his gun while holding his buddy's pointed at him.

Approvingly, Teddy said, "You do that very well."

"Thank you," Raven said politely, sticking the second gun in the waistband of her slacks. "I'm just glad they don't patrol with dogs in the daytime. We could have been bitten or something. We'd better keep an eye on the compound until Josh and the others get here; somebody might get curious and come out to see what's going on."

"Right," Teddy agreed.

Raven gave the soldiers a tiny smile. "On your bellies, guys, arms spread. And try to remember today won't be a good day for heroes, huh?"

"What are we going to do?" Jo asked. "We're locked in here, no weapons, no way out. How can we help?"

Elizabeth's delicate chin rose. "I *won't* just sit and wait to be rescued, dammit! There has to be a way."

She caught sight of something on the floor near the cot, and asked, "What's that?"

Jo looked, shrugged. "A packet of ketchup. It came with one of my lousy meals."

Elizabeth smiled slowly. "I think I have an idea."

"What?" Jo asked, eyeing Elizabeth with foreboding. "Beth, you've got your wild look!"

"Listen, the missile's in the next room, right?"

"Right."

"And it isn't guarded?"

"Doesn't have to be. The whole building's guarded. But Max the maniac is standing by to launch the thing."

Elizabeth remembered the rather wild-eyed man who had been tinkering with the wicked looking missile Thorn had proudly shown her before leading her in here. "Is his mind *totally* on his lethal toy?" she asked.

Jo grinned suddenly. "Are you kidding? He's propositioned me on an average of every other day since Thorn locked me in here. The man's a frustrated playboy."

"Are you afraid of him?" Elizabeth asked searchingly.

"Him? Lord, no. His toy scares the life out of me, but I could handle Max with both my hands tied."

"Good. That's good. And what's a little sacrifice for a worthy cause?"

Jo's eyes narrowed. "What am I going to sacrifice?"

"Your clothes."

"It's been six months since your last inspection, Major Thorn," Kelsey told him briskly. And he was uneasy that Thorn showed no signs of nervousness whatsoever.

"I'm aware of that, Colonel. I am, of course, at your disposal."

"Then let's begin here, shall we?" He gestured to the building they were standing beside. The one that counted.

"Certainly, sir. Sanders, would you—"

"We won't require the lieutenant's company," Kelsey said smoothly, nodding to Thorn's escort. "Just the three of us, Major. I have a few questions."

Thorn's eyes narrowed, but he nodded a dismissal to Lieutenant Sanders, turned, and rapped smartly on the door. There were two cameras poised above the door, both pointed at them, and after a moment the door hissed as it swung open.

"Questions, Colonel?" Thorn inquired as they went inside the building.

Kelsey kept his voice casual. "Later, Major Thorn. I want to see how your operation's set up first."

"The weapons due to be shipped are stored in this building," Thorn explained, leading the way along an aisle between tall stacks of wooden crates.

Kelsey and Zach exchanged a glance, both understanding the significance of that information. No wonder Thorn was undisturbed by their entrance! In this maze of crates he could hide half the building and they'd never miss the space. Unless, that is, his visitors came armed with a little extra information—such as the floor plan drawn by Teddy and Blaine Mallory

Both men set themselves to looking as keenly as possible, searching for the several small rooms secreted away on the north side of the building. And both of them held on tight to their patience as Thorn guided them through the maze.

•　•　•

Jo wiped the ketchup off her arm with a grimace, watching as her sister tugged the guard's limp legs into the room and pushed the door partially closed. "I've never seen you hit anybody before," she noted with interest.

A little pale but determined, Elizabeth tossed Jo's shoe back to her and then bent to remove the guard's holster. Gritting her teeth, she unbuckled his belt. "I never had to. The belt will do for his ankles; find something to tie his arms and gag him, will you, please?"

"How about his shirt? And he probably has a handkerchief."

"Fine. And hurry. I don't think we have much time."

Jo, fascinated by this new side of her sister, knelt and began working the guard out of his shirt. The first part of Elizabeth's plan had gone like clockwork, with the guard responding immediately to Beth's cry that her sister was hurt. A child's trick, of course, but Beth's distress had sounded damned real, and the guard had heard that.

And, Jo reflected, her usually sweet and calm sister had laid that guard out as pretty as you please with a shoe. Beth! And now she was busily binding his ankles as if she'd done things like this all her life.

Jo shook her head, but said, "We could get out of here now, probably."

"Not with Max poised over that missile. If you can distract him long enough for me to get close, I can push him away and hold him off with this gun. Then Kelsey and Derek will only have Thorn to worry about."

Jo sighed. "Him and about thirty soldiers. They're all over the compound, Beth!"

"Thorn can call them off."

"Will he?"

"He will if Kelsey tells him to."

"You have a lot of faith in that man of yours."

Hers. Elizabeth worked to help Jo finish binding the guard's wrists behind his back, her thoughts tangled. He wasn't hers, not really. Maybe not ever. She understood a little better now, what he was.

Despite fear and anxiety, despite the deadly danger posed by Thorn and that missile in the other room, she felt the attraction of danger. Her mind had never worked so clearly as when she had planned this series of moves, and there had been a sense of exhilaration in disabling this professional soldier by using her wits and a well-placed shoe.

And, after fifteen years . . . how could Kelsey give this up? Oh, she could imagine the drawbacks to this brand of dragon slaying—she had heard the pain in Kelsey's voice when he had talked of this father, and knew there had been others lost over the years. And that kind of pain could weigh down even a strong man.

Maybe especially a strong man.

And she thought she could see him now, clearly. She realized, finally, that he was exactly what he appeared to be. A dozen men, maybe a hundred men. He was a part of every role he played, every face he briefly wore, a gifted and instinctive actor who had chosen a deadly stage for his roles.

And no applauding members of the academy offered him a little gold statuette, no grateful studio head offered million dollar contracts to acknowledge his wonderful talent. His face would go unrecognized, his name unknown. Kelsey, a man who could have been anything or anyone he wanted, had simply picked up a sword and gone about the dangerous business of slaying dragons.

"I didn't fit in that world anymore."

Kelsey. Her beloved Kelsey, who honestly didn't know he could fit into any world he chose.

And that was it, really. The bottom line. The role didn't matter—only the performance that was as instinctive to him as breathing. Kelsey would always relish the roles, enjoying each for its own sake . . . because, to him, they *weren't* roles.

They were pieces of himself.

If he chose to fit himself into her world, he would adapt instantly like the chameleon that could have been his namesake. She could see him so clearly in her mind as he went about learning peaches and sisters. Small town life. The responsibilities of a settled home. Maybe a family.

The question was . . . would Kelsey come to terms with himself enough to realize that he *could* fit?

"Beth?"

Jo's voice brought her back to the job at hand, and she shook off the question, knowing that only time and Kelsey could answer it. "Ready?"

Sighing, Jo began removing her clothes. "I can keep on my underwear, can't I?"

"Well, of course. I would never ask my own sister to parade around stark naked in front of a strange maniac!"

"Gee, thanks."

Elizabeth hefted the unfamiliar weight of the gun, studying it uneasily. That was the safety, wasn't it? And this—you pulled this back to—to chamber a round . . . Or, did you? Throwing the matter into the lap of the gods, she took a firm grip on the gun and trusted to luck.

"I'm ready," Jo said.

They left their former guard trussed up neatly, and moved between the wall of crates and the partition which had been erected to shape several small rooms.

"The door isn't locked?" Elizabeth whispered.

"No, never. I go in first, right?"

"Yes. Try to turn him so he faces away from the door—and get him away from the missile if you can."

Jo gave her a mock-haughty look, following her sister's lead in being very calm about all this insanity. "If I can? Hey, Sis, Mata Hari's got nothing on me."

"I hope not," Elizabeth said. "She got shot."

"Great," Jo muttered. It *was* insanity, after all.

Elizabeth turned her head slightly, hearing the rumble of male voices. "Hurry," she urged in a whisper.

Jo took a deep breath, and vanished through the doorway.

Kelsey knew damned well that Thorn was leading them in a carefully thought out, very confusing path through the maze. The trouble was, neither he nor Zach could very well protest until they were sure they knew exactly where they were. Mallory had admitted that Thorn could have shifted the moveable partitions to change the rooms around. He had before.

And then, following along behind Thorn, Kelsey felt Zach touch his arm and followed the other's gaze to see, beyond a tall stack of crates, a faint glimmer of light.

The skylight.

But before they could act, they all three saw a slender figure leaning casually against the crates just ahead. A beautiful blond woman who smiled gently as Thorn stopped dead in the aisle.

"Hello, Major," she said.

And it wasn't very hard, after all, to finish the job. While Thorn was still paralyzed, Kelsey coolly disarmed him and Zach produced a pair of hand cuffs that were put quickly in place.

"Federal and military agents, Major Thorn," Kelsey told him. "You're under arrest."

Zach looked quickly at Elizabeth. "The missile?"

"This way." She led them to the virtually hidden room, and pushed open the door.

And Kelsey knew that never, to his dying day, would be forget the scene presented to him.

A very lovely blond woman stood with a businesslike automatic in one small hand, pointing it steadily at a man who was positioned just a few steps away from a missile.

The man looked less unhappy than he might have under the circumstances, possibly because the lovely lady was naked except for panties and a bra.

Kelsey heard a chuckle from Zach and watched while he moved toward the missile and pulled a small bag of tools from inside his shirt with which to defang a particularly ugly dog of war. And Kelsey was saved from having to remark on the situation when Derek appeared suddenly beside him and firmly took a subdued Thorn's arm.

"Hi," he said casually.

Kelsey stared at him blankly. "How did you get in here?"

"Hell, we own the joint." Derek grinned. "Josh pulled rank, and by the time he explained to the soldiers that their CO was cosying up to a nuclear missile, they were ready to strap him to it and bury them both." He eyed Jo with interest as she came to the door. "Hello."

She smiled at him. "I have clothes around here somewhere."

"Don't find them on my account," he begged politely.

Jo looked at Elizabeth. "Which one is yours?"

"This one," Kelsey said in a low, raspy voice while he reached for Elizabeth's hand.

Jo eyed him. "Yes, of course you are."

"Why don't you get dressed, Jo?" Elizabeth asked, a bit wary of Kelsey's impassive expression.

"Yes, why don't I?" She glared at Thorn, then looked at Derek. "Would you please remove this creature?"

"Yes, ma'am." Derek went in the room quickly to remove Max so that Zach could concentrate on his defanging, then hustled the Major and Max away.

Jo strolled back to her former jail to retrieve her clothes, and her voice sang out a moment later. "There's another one in here, dammit!"

"Tied up," Elizabeth murmured.

Kelsey took a deep breath. "You do realize you could have been killed?" he asked in the calm tone of a man who wanted to get the facts straight.

She nodded. "It occurred to me."

"Then why in hell did you come here?" Kelsey's voice was strained now, thickened. "You knew we were about to move."

"Yes." She looked up at him gravely, her lovely eyes very direct. "I knew. But I didn't know what it felt like to slay a dragon. And I needed to know that, Kelsey."

He looked at her for a moment, then pulled her abruptly into his arms and hugged her. "Dammit," he muttered.

Elizabeth burrowed closer, holding on to what she could of him.

Nine

"A debriefing." Kelsey stood on the bottom step, looking at Elizabeth with restless eyes. "Josh and his crew can get away with just vanishing, but Derek and I have to report in. A few days."

"I understand." She glanced past him, watching a low-slung sports car turn onto the main road from her driveway. "Derek's leaving now?"

Kelsey smiled. "Riding off into the sunset. Like the Lone Ranger."

Elizabeth kept her arms crossed, looking relaxed. The sun was indeed going down. The military men—those who had helped to evacuate Pinnacle—were now in charge of Meditron, with Blaine and Jo remaining there to answer official questions. The missile had been disarmed. Josh Long and his "crew" had departed quietly. The newspapers had yet to hear of the story and, with luck, would find it uninteresting now that the shouting was over.

"Will you drive all night?" she asked steadily.

He shook his head. "Josh pulled a few more strings. I'm meeting Derek in Charleston; there's a military transport waiting for us."

She nodded. "How do I thank you, Kelsey?"

"For what? In the end, I didn't do very much."

"It all happened because of you," she told him quietly. "I never would have found the courage to—to *do* something if it hadn't been for you."

"Elizabeth—"

She lifted a hand to stop him. "You have to be debriefed, remember? We can talk—later."

"I'll be back," he said.

Elizabeth smiled. "I'll be here."

She watched him move slowly to his car and get in. Watched him drive out to the main road and turn toward Charleston. When the sun was gone and the breeze turned chilly, she went inside the house.

The girls would be home soon, she realized. The soldiers hadn't wanted to release any of the citizens—including the students—until they were sure the threat was gone. But now the knew the town was out of danger. They would release the people, and the girls would be home soon. Elizabeth went into the kitchen, turned on lights and began cooking.

When Ami and Meg burst through the front door about an hour later, Elizabeth turned to greet them with a smile.

"Beth!" Ami was flushed and excited. "Soldiers came to school and made us leave. They made the whole town leave!"

"Somebody said there was a bomb," Meg explained. "And we had to wait for *hours* near Charleston in that big park with all the shelters."

"Jo's coming home," Elizabeth said.

Both Ami and Meg went still, their eyes widening.

"From her vacation? Sure," Meg said dismissively.

But Ami's eyes were very bright. "Kelsey did it, didn't he?"

Elizabeth smoothed the fine, pale hair of her youngest sister, and smiled. "Yes. Kelsey did it."

In the cool early morning mist of a spring day, Ami fed the horses and then headed back to the house. She was a little troubled because Kelsey had been gone for over a week now, and Beth had been very quiet. Even Meg, generally not one to notice other people's feelings, had said more than once that "that Kelsey" would be turning up here soon.

But Beth was very quiet.

Ami sighed, then tilted her head as she heard a faint sound from the front of the house. Curious, she walked around from the back, and when she stopped, she could feel her smile growing.

"Hello, Kelsey."

He looked up from his work, smiling in return. "Good morning, little fawn. You're up bright and early."

"The horses," she explained, watching solemnly as he continued working.

"Demanding beasts," he agreed gravely.

"Yes. You've been here awhile."

"It takes time to do this right," he said with a note of apology in his voice.

"I see it does. How long do you want me to wait before I send Beth out?"

He looked up to wink at her. "Give me another half hour, all right?"

"Got it." Ami turned away, then hesitated and looked back at him. "Kelsey?"

He looked up questioningly.

"I'm glad you came back."

Kelsey smiled. "I was always coming back, honey. Elizabeth just didn't know that."

Trying to wipe the silly smile off her face, Ami returned to the house.

And, exactly half an hour later, Elizabeth came out onto the front porch, a puzzled frown on her face. She went very still as soon as she saw, and she stared in wonder.

Lining the front walkway were a dozen rose bushes neatly set out, already budding.

"There isn't a letter."

She turned slowly as Kelsey stepped up onto the porch from the side and regarded her seriously. "Why—why not?" she asked unsteadily, remembering that she had asked him not to send cut roses with the Dear Jane letter.

He stepped closer, his face still grave. And his voice was quiet, reflective. "Because I could never say good-bye to you. I've always known that was true. Even when I didn't know if I could stay here, I knew I could never say good-bye."

Elizabeth took a deep breath. "I realized a few things when I tried my hand at . . . dragon slaying. I realized that it wasn't your fault I wasn't seeing you clearly. You were always there, Kelsey. I just didn't know how to look. But I've learned how to do that. I *can* see you now. And even though I believe you could fit yourself into any life you wanted, I'll still understand if you have to go."

"I resigned from the agency," he said.

Elizabeth could almost hear her heart pounding, and she had to swallow hard.

He smiled tenderly. "Haven't you realized it yet? I'm in love with you."

Her heart caught in her throat, and Elizabeth was in his arms with no memory of moving. He held her tightly, and his voice was husky now, a gentle, rasping sound.

"There's a word for what I feel for you. Stronger than love. Stronger than caring. Stronger than passion."

"What is it?" she whispered.

"Forever. I recognized it from the first, I just didn't understand what it meant. Then I read that note you left, and thought of you in danger. And I understood. *Forever*, Elizabeth. No matter what. No matter where. Nothing else is as strong as that single reality. I'll love you forever."

She lifted her head from his shoulder, and her eyes shone wetly. "That night in your car," she said softly, "when I realized I loved you, that's what I felt. That, no matter what happened, I'd always love you. Even if you left me. I never had a choice."

He framed her face in warm hands and kissed her, a gentle touch that rapidly became something fierce. Lifting his head at last, he said somewhat hoarsely, "I hope you don't mind, but I'm planning on all the proper flourishes for this relationship. Starting with an engagement ring and very quickly followed by a wedding."

Elizabeth gazed up at him lovingly. "Oh . . . I think I can live with that. But are you sure?"

"I've never been more certain of anything in my life," he responded, and the truth of his words was in the fervent tone of his voice.

She kissed him. "We should tell the girls," she murmured.

"*Tell* us?" a voice exclaimed from the door, where Jo stood with Ami and Meg at her side. "You think we're blind or something?"

Epilogue

Hagen studied the coded message in his hands for a long time, then methodically tore the paper into tiny pieces.

He burned the pieces in a brass ashtray.

Then, almost idly, he said to the empty room, "I suppose it could be considered kidnapping. But, maybe not. And I do owe the man a favor."

He sighed.

And he sat for a long time in the silent office, thinking about Kadeira.

THE EDITOR'S CORNER

It's not easy handling six spirited heroines and six "to die for" handsome, sexy heroes each month, but it's fun trying. It's a tough job, but someone has to do it! The truth is there's nothing tough about editing these LOVESWEPTs—our authors are a joy to work with. What's tough is knowing which book to read first! Luckily, we've solved that problem for you by numbering the books. So once again we have six books that explore romance in all its forms—steamy, sensuous, sweet, funny, and heartwarming.

Our first LOVESWEPT for the month, #240 **CAJUN NIGHTS** by Susan Richardson is definitely steamy! It's set in the bayous of Louisiana where our heroine, renowned travel writer Jeannie Kilmartin, is looking for the perfect hideaway for her next story. Instead, she finds dark, brooding Elliot Escudier poling through the water on his handmade boat. Jeannie has to look twice as Elliot appears in the marshes—is he some long lost pirate who's come to claim her? Elliot owns the land that Jeannie is writing about and he's come to claim the land and keep her from printing her article. And he'll do anything to stop her. Jeannie doesn't mind his interference because she adores his dark, sexy looks. Eventually, all thoughts of an article are thrown out the window when the lovers finally succumb to their overwhelming desire.

In **TRAVELIN' MAN** by Charlotte Hughes, LOVESWEPT #241, Dannie Drysdale is whimsical and luscious looking and utterly determined not to fall in love with a traveling man because at last she's put down roots. Brian Anthony is one extraordinary fellow—as handsome as he is sensitive! But alas, he's a salesman on the move who's determined to rise to the top of the corporate ladder. Nothing can stand in his way or keep him in one place for long. Except Dannie! Once Dannie's eccentric father throws the lovers together, Brian's goals change. Then Dannie's resistance is finally broken down by a bad case of chickenpox and by the great guy who's nursing her back to health. The travelin' man and the

(continued)

"stay-put" woman realize that they both want the same thing—each other!

Something funny happened at LOVESWEPT this month—we discovered we had two heroes with the same name. You probably think that the hero's name is John or Joe or Tom, Dick or Harry—a common name that could easily be duplicated. But then you know that our heroes are never common so they never have common names. Can you believe that we have two strong, sexy, devastating Lincolns this month? Well, we do and we'll let you decide which one is more lovable, but we know that's going to be a very tough decision.

In **INTIMATE DETAILS,** by Barbara Boswell, LOVE-SWEPT #242, Lincoln Scott is the man Vanessa Ramsey's father decides she should marry. Lincoln finds the dazzling temptress a delectable challenge, especially since she won't consider even liking Linc—and her father's interference has turned her into a tigress! But Vanessa finds it harder and harder to ignore Lincoln's dreamboat looks and his fierce caresses. When he touches her heart, Vanessa listens to her feelings and for the first time in her life, she lets herself be loved. There are some of Barbara's wittiest scenes in this delightful love story—such as one in which her father tries to justify his actions and digs himself into a hole a mile deep. Unforgettable.

Joan Elliott Pickart's offering for the month is **KISS ME AGAIN, SAM,** LOVESWEPT #243, a wonderfully humorous and heartwarming romance in which the heroine appears for the first time hanging from the rafters! Read on and find out how she got there and you'll discover that Austin Tyler is a very pretty auburn-haired construction worker hired to repair Sam Carter's house. Sam finds Austin irresistible in both body and mind and he tells her so. But Austin is afraid that once she tells Sam her terrible secret, he won't want her anymore. Could he make her believe that everything about her was precious to him and he loved all the woman she was?

SAPPHIRE LIGHTNING by Fayrene Preston, LOVE-SWEPT #244 features our second hero named Linc and I must admit I'm torn between the two men! Linc Sinclair

(continued)

is a handsome, healthy jogger with a fantastic body, as well as being a successful businessman with a fabulous art collection. Toni Sinclair was married to his cousin who died accidentally and now that Toni is on her own with her six-month-old son, she's decided never to remarry. She wasn't a great wife the first time around, and she doesn't want to risk failing again. Linc throws a party in her honor welcoming Toni to the family's hometown and while at his house, Toni realizes just how much they have in common. It all begins with a love for art—and ends with Linc's love for one particular beautiful, female artist. Fayrene Preston has once again set a sensuous, romantic scene where two lovers destined for one another will be sure to find their hearts' desires.

Deborah Smith is a new LOVESWEPT author and we're very excited about **JED'S SWEET REVENGE**, LOVESWEPT #245, the story of a sun-bronzed cowboy and the beautiful woman he calls "Wildflower"! Jed Powers leaves Wyoming and heads south for Sancia Island to finally seek his revenge on his dead grandfather. Instead he finds Thena Saint-Colbet—very much alive and a gorgeous free spirit with wild, thick auburn hair. Thena lives on the island that Jed intends to destroy, and she teaches him its beauty. All thought of revenge fades when love takes its place and, in the end, Jed's revenge is sweet.

I'm sure you're going to enjoy Deborah Smith's book and welcome her to the LOVESWEPT family. You have a wonderful month of reading ahead of you, so stay warm and cozy with your favorite LOVESWEPT.

Sincerely,

Kate Hartson

Kate Hartson
    Editor
LOVESWEPT
Bantam Books, Inc.
666 Fifth Avenue
New York, NY 10103

HANDSOME, SPACE-SAVER
BOOKRACK

ONLY
$9.95

Nevco US Pat. 3,464,565

Perfect as a desk or table top library— Holds both hardcovers and paperbacks.

- hand-rubbed walnut finish
- patented sturdy construction
- assembles in seconds
- assembled size 16" x 8"

The first Delaney trilogy

*Heirs to a great dynasty, the Delaney
brothers were united by blood, united by
devotion to their rugged land . . . and
known far and wide as*

THE SHAMROCK
TRINITY

Bantam's bestselling LOVESWEPT romance line built its reputation on quality and innovation. Now, a remarkable and unique
event in romance publishing comes from the same source: THE
SHAMROCK TRINITY, three daringly original novels written by
three of the most successful women's romance writers today. Kay
Hooper, Iris Johansen, and Fayrene Preston have created a trio
of books that are dynamite love stories bursting with strong,
fascinating male and female characters, deeply sensual love scenes,
the humor for which LOVESWEPT is famous, and a deliciously
fresh approach to romance writing.

*THE SHAMROCK TRINITY—Burke, York, and
Rafe: Powerful men . . . rakes and charmers . . .
they needed only love to make their lives complete.*

☐ RAFE, THE MAVERICK by Kay Hooper

Rafe Delaney was a heartbreaker whose ebony eyes held laughing
devils and whose lilting voice could charm any lady—or any
horse—until a stallion named Diablo left him in the dust. It took
Maggie O'Riley to work her magic on the impossible horse . . .
and on his bold owner. Maggie's grace and strength made Rafe
yearn to share the raw beauty of his land with her, to teach her
the exquisite pleasure of yielding to the heat inside her. Maggie
was stirred by Rafe's passion, but would his reputation and her
ambition keep their kindred spirits apart?   (21846 • $2.75)

LOVESWEPT

☐ YORK, THE RENEGADE by Iris Johansen

Some men were made to fight dragons, Sierra Smith thought when she first met York Delaney. The rebel brother had roamed the world for years before calling the rough mining town of Hell's Bluff home. Now, the spirited young woman who'd penetrated this renegade's paradise had awakened a savage and tender possessiveness in York: something he never expected to find in himself. Sierra had known loneliness and isolation too—enough to realize that York's restlessness had only to do with finding a place to belong. Could she convince him that love was such a place, that the refuge he'd always sought was in her arms?

(21847 • $2.75)

☐ BURKE, THE KINGPIN by Fayrene Preston

Cara Winston appeared as a fantasy, racing on horseback to catch the day's last light—her silver hair glistening, her dress the color of the Arizona sunset . . . and Burke Delaney wanted her. She was on his horse, on his land: she would have to belong to him too. But Cara was quicksilver, impossible to hold, a wild creature whose scent was midnight flowers and sweet grass. Burke had always taken what he wanted, by willing it or fighting for it; Cara cherished her freedom and refused to believe his love would last. Could he make her see he'd captured her to have and hold forever?

(21848 • $2.75)